Olive Press
Suite 3.3
84 Barrland Street
Glasgow
G41 1RJ

The Last Libertine first published by Olive Press in 2012

ISBN: 978-1-4750-9864-8

For Aimee

राधा
हरे कृष्ण

Michael Q. Black

For Amitee

ग़ालि

कही सुना

कृषक मीत

The Last Libertine:

A 21st Century Gonzo Odyssey

Michael Q. Black

1. A Bad Trip In A West Coast State…

We were heading down Lincoln Boulevard when the Rabbi spoke.

"Dude, you look like fuckin' crap!"

His eyes were back on the road ahead and the sudden return to his previous calm composure made me feel relaxed and uneasy at the same time. There was no telling what the crazy bastard was likely to do when he got excitable.

"There's a bottle of Bourbon in the back to take the edge off if you need it," he added.

"Thanks man. It's good to see you too. How's your kid?"

I picked up the bottle resting on the back seat next to the baby booster. It worried me.

"I had a swig before coming into the airport… the kid's great. You know what they say. They grow up so fast. He'll soon be getting to that age where girls will start taking notice of him. He'll be fighting them off with sticks!"

There was almost a hint of fatherly pride in his voice. He paused before he said his next words.

"Oh, Bella was asking for you."

Bella? The name rang a bell in the back of my mind, but I couldn't place the face. Then it hit me. That night in New York.

"So tell me about this girl that had you all whacked," he said.

"You mean Kandy? I don't know man. She's a weird one. She's got this way about her that makes my head cry havoc."

"Yeah? That's women for you. They drive you crazy then burn a hole in your pockets. I met a girl like that this year. American girls are the worst for that. They look at the size of your wallet more than the size of your shoes."

"Why should that prove a problem for you? You've got a

big wallet and take a size 12," I said, genuinely confused by the nature of his concern.

"Bro, haven't you been keeping up with the markets? Stuff is crashing everywhere. The God business isn't as good as it used to be. That's why I had to turn to making those films. But even that isn't raking it in like before. I'm getting freaked out a little. It's not just about the chiquitas. I've got to think about my son's future too."

He was right. Things were changing for everyone. The economy we were all used to was built on infinite inflation and unregulated debt. It was doomed to failure the moment the idea was hatched in the mind of an economic sex-freak who'd fucked the public without adequate protection. Absolute power, granted to bankers who cooked their books to make the markets look as good as risk free Thai hookers. They enticed passing clientele with their empty promises of happy endings. Right in the middle of this global cluster-fuck of corruption was my friend, getting rammed like everyone else who had nickels and dimes put away for rainy days. I had no such troubles; it was the upside of having nothing.

"Don't worry buddy. Things will get better," I said, knowing full well that the system of old was teetering on the edge of inevitable destruction.

"So the girl…" he was quick to change to subject.

"What? Oh yeah. Her. Well, she's a real hottie, a real Rita Hayworth type. I was thinking about giving her my plant."

"You were gonna give her your plant?! Shit, it must have been love!"

His words faded into the darkness as my eyelids got heavy and I began to drift off, deep into the nightmare of modern living.

Just a few hours earlier I was at the mercy of three very large burger loving fat fuckers, in the gainful employ of their

President and country. At first glance, they looked moderately respectable in their smart uniforms, but my psychic perceptions told me they were related to Freddy Kruger. Little did I know that I would be proved correct.

"Mr Blotnik?"

"Yes?"

"Mr Maxwell Qasim Blotnik?"

"Yes, that's me."

"You've been selected for a body cavity search, sir," said the man at the immigration check point. "Could you step over to the left? These gentlemen will escort you to the appropriate area."

I was quickly hauled into a private room and watched in horror as they donned the glove of evil. There was no doubt left as to the intentions of these hell-spawn. They talked quietly amongst themselves for a few short moments while I waited in a tiny, hermetically sealed room. I heard them laugh as one fellow grabbed me by the collar and threw my shell shocked body against a wall.

"We know all about *your* kind. We don't want them coming over. But we *do* know to treat you people right. We're going to help you get used to the way things are done here. Agent C?"

"Our computer and camera system selected you for screening. Your behaviour has raised concerns, and as required by the subsections of the P.A.T.R.I.O.T. Act, we will have to carry out the necessary checks," said agent C, grinning.

He made it sound like I'd won a prize at the carnival. It was true, I had been acting jittery and was sweating like an Algerian camel's balls; this was because of my predilection for Southern Comfort; I was dehydrated and a nervous flier, I told them, but it did no good. In their eyes, I fit the profile of a Colombian drug baron, or perhaps a Tahitian terrorist; some freak who shoved a bomb up his ass to cause an explosion in his pants. This dangerous assumption led them to the conclusion that I would enjoy the perverse experience that would follow. I panicked in a moment of temporary sanity.

"Thus I clothe my naked villainy with old odd ends!" I blurted.

Things were clearly bad if my subconscious was quoting Shakespeare. The Big Mac loving pig-men were intent on exploring my every orifice; all without applying lubrication. I'd heard it said that even the devil used spit before ramming his pitchfork into unfortunate sinners. I wondered how long the terrible torment would continue. In just under twenty hours of travel time by plane, train and auto mobile, I had been scanned, searched, fingerprinted and finger-fucked; by not one, but three massive mammoths. Regardless of the depths their depravity would now sink to, it was already past the point of decency.

This was America, the land of the free. But the free had all been caught and caged; to *protect* them from harming themselves. Civil liberties pioneered by this home of the brave were being betrayed, shredded and shot out of the flint pistol once fired for freedom. In two-thousand and eleven, Martin Luther King's dream was still going strong. But three years after the change in the Whitehouse colour scheme, the whitewash remained the same. The dream was in danger of becoming little more than a hallucination - a hangover from decades' worth of magic mushroom induced highs.

Even now, corruption was thriving in every tier of each political establishment; and it overshadowed any sexual scandal involving Monica Lewinsky. In both Capitol Hill and Westminster, rent boys were being hired out to politicians and press packers alike, in exchange for lucrative oiled-up back room deals. These thoroughly abused young things - wealth and power -

were too seductive for any of our self-serving representatives to turn down. It didn't take long before servants of the state were following their masters' lead.

"Excuse the inconvenience, sir. Just follow the signs toward the exit. Your friend is waiting for you at arrivals. *Everything* checked out just fine," said Agent C, smiling with smug satisfaction.

Was he making some kind of veiled reference to our private session of 'find the drug filled condom'? I scowled at him as he and his white devil minions threw me out of the search booth.

I grabbed my suitcase from the baggage claim and tried not to dwell on what had just transpired. Rabbi Glassman was indeed waiting. I was glad to see him. He smiled. It was one of those smiles that brought with it a feeling of reassurance and warmth, infectiously encompassing everyone in its path. It added to his natural film-star good looks and inherent charm. His set and permed hair gave him the appearance of a man who idled away his Sunday afternoons playing golf and enjoying the benefits of the club steam room. But this was far from the truth. The Rabbi was a workhorse. When he wasn't saving lost sheep, he was busy cranking out homemade movie projects aimed at Hollywood's elite. That was his ambition, to become a fully fledged avant-garde film-maker. It was one of the many reasons why he and I had become such close friends.

We glanced at the cosmetic surgery addicts to our left. The older of the two - easily in her fifties - squealed in a high pitched shriek that almost burst my eardrums. She sat next to me on the final leg of my journey and I found her to be as air-headed as a balloon. The Rabbi looked her up and down, checked the junk in her trunk and turned back to me. I hadn't seen the iconic letch in over three years - not since that fateful night - and here we were, just like old times, assessing the intricate work that went into breast implants; agreeing that it was a testament to the practical application of modern science.

We headed out to the car park where he'd parked his gas guzzling Mercedes SUV. He never purchased American cars and never bought small. It was his 'fuck you' to the concept of carbon taxation without representation. I understood his frustrations. While I was in favour of environmental awareness, taxes that went into the pockets of corrupt financiers did nothing to bring harmony to Mother Earth. People still burned through oil as if it was sweet water flowing down from Mount Olympus. We were still waging wars for a finite substance, to keep the wheels greased on the road to El Dorado; killing for plastic; illogically killing to produce the logical computer.

I basked in the warm Californian sun as we drove toward the Rabbi's fortified castle and woke just as he pulled up to his mansion on Admiral Avenue. The Marina Del Rey, a secluded sanctuary for those who could afford the safe shelter within its confines. The hired help took care of my belongings while the Rabbi and I took a stroll around the garden and pool area. To say it was beautiful would have been an understatement. It was magnificent; opulence incarnate. The marina itself was close by, where avid water sport enthusiasts tested their skill and luck against the forces of nature.

"I was going to keep this a secret, but I'm throwing a pool party tonight. Sort of in your honour. I know how you hate surprises, so I thought I'd best tell you," he said.

"I don't know what to say man. I'm touched. Though I do hate things being sprung on me."

As the evening air got cooler, we took refuge indoors. He showed me to the guest bedroom and I examined the area for roaches and other bugs, of which I had a paralysing phobia. I shot him a look of intense disapproval after seeing the floral bed sheets that almost matched my summer shirt.

"They were not my idea! Mom did the sheets in here. You know she thinks of you as a second son. Nothing but the best for my brother from another mother!"

"I'm flattered," I said. "How is the old battleaxe?"

"She's great. She's here. You can say hi once you've freshened up. I'll be in the den. Got some stuff to finish up on the editing front."

He left the room and I rummaged through the case to locate my shaving kit, packed next to a pair of unopened tennis socks. I crept toward the bathroom, unworn clothes in hand, hoping to wash off the stains marking my psyche from the earlier unpleasantness. Eventually, after getting lost and ending up in various broom cupboards and closets, I found the wash room. It was bigger than my entire flat back in Scotland. I was awed by the spectacular sight. The sheer dimensions were astonishing. There was a hot tub installed in the centre, with more knobs and controls than a NASA space shuttle. I spotted some clean towels on the shelf next to the door. Eight in total; four large bath-towels, two hand towels and two that were a size somewhere in between.

2. A Holy Man In The City of Angels...

An hour and a plethora of bubbles later, I emerged from the tank like the Loch Ness Monster. I'd made it to L.A. in one piece; not unscathed; but at least with most of my sanity intact. My mind had been taken off the emotional upheavals that led to this unplanned exodus. But I knew this sense of peacefulness was not going to last. I got dressed and made my way to the den where I was sure I'd find the Rabbi hard at work. Instead, I came upon his mother Golda, painting her fingernails with purple nail-varnish.

"Max-well!"

She always added that inflection to the end of my name.

"Avi went to go fetch a few things for his party tonight."

Momma Glassman gave me a bone-crunching hug and pinched and kissed my cheeks.

"It's so good to see you! It has been too long. How are you? What have you been doing with yourself? Why have you been away so long?"

I didn't have the heart to tell her the truth. Being poverty stricken and without a pot to piss in is not something you can boast about as a prodigal son. I remembered the first time the Rabbi had introduced me to his family and friends. I'd overheard Golda and the Rabbi speaking afterwards. Her words echoed in my ears as I stood there, dumbstruck. "I have a lot of faith in that boy, Avi. He's got the same grit and determination in his eyes that I saw in you as a young man. You must look out for him."

Avi had looked out for me. But how could I explain to her that I had no job, no future, no girlfriend, and that I was about as far from having any of those as I could get? I didn't want to disappoint her. The last time I'd seen her I was only one item shy on that laundry list of deficits, and at the time, it wasn't a priority.

Women came and went and in those years. I never had to wait long between one girl and the next. It was a lot easier to get laid than to get loved.

"I've been busy," I replied.

I rubbed my neck in that awkward way you do when you've accidentally shot your neighbours goldfish bowl with an illegally obtained handgun. But even that was easier to deal with than the interrogating laser-beam gaze of a Jewish mother.

Just then, I heard a car pull up on the gravel-spread driveway. Voices murmured and squabbled, getting ever closer. I recognised one. The other seemed familiar too, but I couldn't place it.

"Oy Vey! Are you going to make me carry *all* of this inside? Give me a hand dammit!"

I was about to run and help when I realised that the request wasn't directed at me. The Rabbi kicked the swing door open and walked in with boxes in each hand. Behind him was a woman; the same woman who'd been complaining endlessly outside. The Rabbi's six-foot frame moved over to the desk and I could now see her face. My heart got stuck in my throat. It was Bella.

"Hi," she said, not moving.

The Rabbi took the bags from her hands. I stared at her for a while before replying. My mouth was dry and I barely mustered a response.

"Hi," I paused for a few seconds, unsure of what to say next. "You look great."

"Thanks. You too. How was your flight?"

"Long," I said.

The Rabbi emptied the boxes he'd brought in. Everything from Bell's whiskey to fine South African wine lined the length and breadth of the table. I helped him fold down the boxes and she did the same. It was safe to say that Bella was one of the few women who had once loved me, but being immature and irresponsible, I had no clue as to the real value of love in those days. I was careless and inconsiderate with her feelings, playing fast and loose with that cavalier attitude most jaded people carry with them. Whatever may have been between us was dead in the water quicker than a harpooned sperm whale off the coast of Japan.

The four of us shared a quiet drink on the patio and enjoyed the benefits of good circulation in the great outdoors. The Rabbi suggested bringing out the gas barbecue, stowed in the garage for the better part of that year. Bella and I thought it was a stellar idea and helped him drag it out from under a mountain of collected junk. It looked like something Satan had constructed on his day off, for the specific purpose of roasting Stalin's iron testicles. Fire-apple red. Golda paid us little attention. She was busy reading her copy of Vogue magazine and relaxing with a Long Island Ice Tea by her side.

Hooking up the gas tank was easy and didn't take much effort. We raided the larder for meat to splay across the heavy duty industrial grill. I ducked out of the house with my arms full of packaged meat, cradling a heap of lamb chops, steaks and marinated chicken breasts. It occurred to me that the Rabbi had likely pre-planned for such an occasion but hadn't quite gotten around to hoisting out the flame-spewing grilling machine.

Guests began to arrive just as we were organizing the evening's entertainment. The Rabbi brought out his boom box from the den and we piled his CD collection into an old wheelbarrow and carted it out, placing it beside the pool. This, we figured, would leave the choice of music in the hands of the attendees and not down to the three of us. All of us had eclectic tastes which were not appreciated by the general public. Bella had flirted with industrial music for a while and learned to appreciate the incessant bashing of used oil drums against steel toe capped boots. My own ears were terminally tuned into the sounds of the seventies and rarely ventured into the realms of new age pop. The Rabbi could listen to just about anything; but his own preferences were a matter of Californian folklore. Johnny Cash, Perry Como and Roy Orbison. These were the three lightening rods that kept him grounded.

"The pool cleaner has been around this afternoon!" announced the Rabbi, "Please feel free to take a dip. Even if you didn't bring a bathing suit!"

Imbibing was promoted and mischief was compulsory. Contrary to outward appearances, Rabbi Glassman was not the straight-laced religious scholar he liked to portray himself as. The moment no-one was watching, he clawed out of his buttoned down professional garments and dived into a pair of Bermuda shorts that hung down to his knees. He was like Superman in this regard; a man with dual identities; with his own flash superhero costume to boot.

I asked about his son. I hadn't seen the little devil since my arrival and I was concerned, especially with all the alcohol that was flowing more freely than a retired pensioner's bladder.

"He's staying over at his mom's tonight," he said. "I'm footloose and free! Free for a day!"

He and his wife had parted ways almost a year after the kid was born. It was a sad state of affairs. He'd gotten custody of their son when she was deemed an unfit parent by the state of California. The primary basis for the judge's decision was the initially undisclosed fact that she had overdosed on a speed-ball in a downtown drug den in the middle of a school day. She checked into rehab subsequently and went through court ordered detox; but it took Avi many years to build up a workable relationship with her; one where they shared parental responsibility. Neither he nor Golda completely trusted her. I noted that the Rabbi checked his phone with regularity throughout the evening.

Avi's religious enlightenment came on the eve of his son's second birthday. Up until then, his main focus and port through every storm had been the health and fitness kick he'd been on since his twenties. He was a fully fledged exercise nut and worked out every day of the week, except on Shabbat. He even hired out his services as a personal trainer. Given his physique, it wasn't surprising that the majority of his clients were women and he relished offering them his 'extra special work out sessions'. It was during one of these that his son had been conceived. Before his spawn turned two, he experienced what addicts often refer to as 'an instant of clarity'. He began to recognize that there was something missing within him, and he became driven by a need to search for that something. Two trips to Egypt, a short stay in the holy land and a slew of eastern mystics later, he claimed to know the secrets of the hidden universe, becoming a teacher to countless lost souls - all desperate for answers.

A total of about fifty or sixty people had gathered around his not-so-humble home. I only knew a handful, and most of them only in passing. But the Rabbi certainly knew how to throw a party. The meat on the grill went down well and we had a blast charring the hell out of orders from people we didn't like. Even a live rock band put in an appearance and belted out a tune or two.

Golda was talking her son up to every young lady within five yards of earshot.

"I want to see you settle down with a *nice* girl Avi," she'd tell him, "You deserve a *good* Jewish girl who'll look after you. Stop wasting your time on these *shiksas*!"

More people came, and with them more bottles; many with homemade kick-ass concoctions. I sampled some moonshine that was doing the rounds.

"It's a hundred and sixty proof! Try it, it'll put hairs on your chest!" said the man with the jug.

"You can't get a hundred and sixty proof," I said, "besides; I already have a ferret's pelt on my chest."

"Doesn't matter. Take a swig. Trust me, this will make you into a sexual Tyrannosaurus!" he exclaimed.

I spent the next hour bowlegged and babbling like a baboon, extolling the virtues of Salman Rushdie's Satanic Verses to a conservative Iranian. He'd only come over to complain about the noise.

He declared me an infidel so I chased him to his car, armed with a large kebab skewer. Technically, he was correct. I had no time for orthodox religion. But I was far from an infidel and was deeply offended by his pronouncement. I believed in the unified beginnings of all creation, a sort of collective consciousness of all living things. This was my God, heavy duty tree of life stuff. The Rabbi's teachings had re-affirmed those beliefs.

Bella was standing next to me, shaking her head vigorously. I hid the skewer behind my back and smiled at her.

"You haven't changed one bit!" she laughed.

"Should I have?" I asked.

"No. I like you just the way you are. You're like Rasputin, except way crazier!"

"Yeah. But sadly I'm not banging the Queen. Then again, I don't think I'd want to. Queen Elizabeth is getting on a bit these days!"

We rejoined the Rabbi; though he was busy sampling a Bundt cake brought over by a German couple. In the distance, close to the rose bushes, I could see Divine and Mario, old friends from the valley. Divine certainly was a beautiful creature and a free spirit; a goddess among mere mortal women, with huge natural tits and a big ass begging to be coveted. Any man on earth would have robbed every bank in the United States and laid it at her feet, just to taste her sweetness. Many already had. But she now only had eyes for Mario, the polished Italian stallion with 1200cc's of horsepower between his legs. His Ducati was a work of art; a real crowd pleaser. He strode up and gave me one of his custom macho man hugs.

"Max! When I heard you were in town, I thought to myself, 'I must go and see him'. Divine and I were just talking about you the other day. I still owe you for that favour," he said.

I looked over his shoulder.

"Divine! So good to see you!"

"And you sweetie! We were so excited. It's been forever!" she said, hitting me lightly with her handbag. "Next time, don't leave it so long!"

"I won't."

We sampled the champagne and chatted for a while. By the end of the night, no-one was sober. We lit some fireworks - leftovers from the fourth of July – and stared at the moon, howling loudly at three am. Golda had already retired for the night and the Rabbi urged us to avoid waking her. At first, I thought he was just being a concerned son, but I soon realised this was not the case. Mario took out a small pipe, some tin foil and a seven gram rock. Crack cocaine was a vice I generally didn't indulge in, and certainly never in Glasgow. I'd read about dealers cutting it with drain cleaner or various household chemicals that could send a man to his grave. But being in trusted company, and knowing that Mario only bought from a reputable source, I decided to partake.

High and horny, things quickly descended into a chaotic frenzy. Clothes were stripped and ripped off and unfettered tongues explored pink flesh and lusciously erect nipples. Men were screwing men, women were topping women, and dogs were mating cats. Fluids gushed forth like Niagara Falls and nothing was left that hadn't been ravished. It was as though the Romans were ransacking the West Coast in a revival of Pompeii's finest moments.

By sun-up I was in the guest room with no memory of how I'd gotten there. Only remnants of decaying flashbacks were left. I couldn't bring myself to leave for the better part of an hour, too afraid of what and who I'd encounter if I ventured outside. When eventually I did, I found that not a single soul remained save the Rabbi and me. The pool was a complete mess, the floors inside were covered in mud and a giant moose head had been placed on top of the toilet seat in the bathroom. I wasn't thrilled at prospect of having a dead animal stare at me as I took a leak, so I carried it out into the yard where Avi was sunning himself on a lawn chair. I crept up behind him, dropped the moose head on his six-pack abs and ran back into the bathroom.

"You bastard! You evil fucking bastard! I'll get you for that!"

For a while, I was worried that he might retaliate. But I didn't hear anything and assumed that it was safe to take a crap without fear of being disturbed. This was sibling rivalry taken to hideous extremes, but such was our relationship. Avi had pulled me out of more lows than anyone. He'd saved my neck more than once. After my depressive episode in New York City, he was the one who fronted me the money for a plane ticket back to Scotland. He knew my salvation lay in going back to my roots of thirteen years and not in hospitalization. "A cactus can only grow in the desert, not in a paddy field. America is a paddy field.' he said. I had no idea what the hell he meant, but I went anyway.

3. Counting Kcals In California...

At 1.30pm, settled and more awake, the Rabbi suggested we meet Bella for lunch at the most happening restaurant in town. Mr Chow's was known for its showcased menu, high-end prices and celebrity diners. I wasn't sure that we'd get in given our propensity for making trouble and my slightly tight budget, but the Rabbi said this would not be a problem.

"Relax," he said. "The Lord and I have an understanding. We'll get in. I'd better call Bella and tell her our plans."

We cruised in comfort thanks to the Rabbi's air-conditioned car. Tourists were huddled like ants around the Hollywood walk of fame. I was tempted to get out and circle the block. It would have been easy to draw a crowd. They all *expected* to encounter famous people and I knew could fool them all with my Don Johnson style of attire and designer sunglasses. The fools didn't know that most persons in the public eye were safely tucked away, enclosed within the confines of tall walls, watching reruns of Jeopardy. That was, of course, until some freelancing, chancing paparazzi got through the net of necessitated precautions. It was a dreadful cycle. I'd been unlucky enough to meet some of those self obsessed 'stars' on my previous visit. I was not impressed.

"Hey, you wanna go to the Universal theme park?" asked the Rabbi.

"What for? It was fun the last time, but I doubt I'd get the same kick out of it again," I replied.

It was obvious he was in the process of planning activities for the rest of my vacation. He knew I needed to take my mind off the stress I'd escaped from. The valet was on standby outside Mr Chows. We got out of the vehicle and the Rabbi threw him the keys. "You scratch it, you go six feet under!"

The doorman peered over his list of pre-booked patrons.

"I don't see you on the list, sir."

Avi stared straight into his eyeballs, burning a hole into the other man's retinas.

"Perhaps it's under the name of the other gentleman in your party. What did you say your name was?" he asked nervously, looking to me for help.

"They call me Mister Tibbs!" I replied, doing my best Sidney Poitier impression.

"Look," said the Rabbi, "we're friends of the management! Now, unless you want to get fired, you'd better let us in. Do we not look like upstanding respectable gentleman to you? You don't want to be branded an anti-Semite do you? Are you bigoted?"

"Let me check again…" he gulped, "yes, I believe we have an opening. Table six. The maitre d' will guide you to it."

A sleek Chinese man showed us the way, seated us at the table and handed us a wine list and a menu. The first was not a wise move. I was still in the process of recovering from my hangover. But the Rabbi insisted that it would do me good to add ballast to my light-headedness. I stared out of the window and saw nothing but pink elephants. As I turned, I spotted Bella talking to the doorman. She pointed at us and waved. The doorman nodded and let her in. She strutted up to the table and ran her fingers through her short jet-black hair.

"I can't believe you got in here!" she squealed.

"Neither can we," I said, looking at the Rabbi who was ready to order.

A waiter brought another menu over. Bella glanced at it and put it down quickly. She asked Avi to order for her. He chose an expensive Claret, three appetizers, four main courses and four desserts.

The waiter opened the wine bottle and handed Avi the cork

to admire its bouquet. The Rabbi sniffed it while the man in the red waistcoat poured a sample into a wineglass. Avi swirled the vino around in the glass and then tasted it. I could hear it swishing as it circled his palate. He gave it a resounding thumbs-up and the waiter poured the blood-red liquid for each of us before placing the bottle in the centre of our table.

The spring rolls, quail eggs and carrot soup didn't take long to arrive, but the crab, sliced seaweed and calamari was not dished out in good time, so I excused myself to use the restroom. I wandered by the kitchen and couldn't resist the temptation to take a peek. I peered through the small window panel on the swing door and saw one of the trainee chefs preparing some egg fried rice and Chop Sui. His colleague was hunched over another plate. At first it was difficult to tell what he was doing. Then I saw. There he was, in broad daylight, fornicating with a plate of jellied eels. His eyes rolled back and a smattering of thick fluid covered the contents. I was not put off eating, however, as he was not the cook assigned to our orders. But I did feel a sense of revulsion on behalf of those who'd have to enjoy his handy work.

The restrooms were just past the kitchen. They were amongst the cleanest I'd ever seen, with the most polite toilet attendant I'd had the pleasure of encountering. He dried my hands with a fresh towel and spritzed me with some aftershave or other. I gave him ten dollars, thanked him and told him to carry on flying the flag for capitalism.

The wank-happy chef walked by me as I made my way back to the table. I saw him ask an old Frenchman if he'd enjoyed his meal. Bella was telling the Rabbi about her new diet. She could eat anything she wanted and not put an inch on her waistline. I gazed down at my bulging gut, then at the two picture-perfect bodies next to me. On and on she droned, lecturing me on the benefits of juniper berries, guava juice and fruitarian pear farms. I was not remotely interested. But the Rabbi was entranced.

"Well. There's always the tapeworm diet," I interjected.

"No way! I'd never do that. Why swallow a tapeworm when all you have to do is count your calories?" said Bella.

"Anyone want to take a guess how many Kcals are in what we've just ordered?" asked the Rabbi.

"So, Bella, how was your day?"

"It was good," she replied, "I went jogging down Sunset Strip earlier before picking the brain of an old school Hollywood diva I bumped into. What a trip; she'd forgotten even more than she remembered!"

"That'll happen if you keep Barbara Walters whacked on roofies and chained in the basement," I said. "There's bound to be some permanent damage over time."

"She's not chained in the basement," she chuckled. "I keep her in the attic stoned on psilocybin."

"Dear God! Have you no shame?" I said. "These Hollywood types... they just aren't prepared for the sort of madness that can cause. We real people might cope with images of Japanese sumo wrestlers humping our eye sockets; but can you imagine what that kind of hallucination would do to one of *them*? They'd run amok, stealing sausages from other old ladies in grocery stores!"

The Rabbi nearly choked on his sorbet, but I was ready and prepared to perform the Heimlich manoeuvre if it came to it. Bella doubled over with a fit of the giggles. Tears were streaming down her face and she went beet red. But she wasn't one to be beaten, not even in this surreal session of verbal jousting.

"It's not like I don't look after her. I had the doctor over. He said there was a chance it could lead to early onset of Alzheimer's. Actually, she's a very sweet lady, normally or running amok," she parried.

"Alzheimer's eh? I wonder if that would explain her satanic sex orgies with John Warner and Alan Greenspan. Personally I think she's the greatest patriot in history; I mean Greenspan! Only someone who really loved their country could go there," I said.

I wondered if Bill Clinton, America's greatest love machine, had ever hired Walters to polish the Whitehouse flagpole. The Rabbi was in hysterics and Bella was gasping for air. The Maitre d' shot us a look of utter contempt and told us that we were making the other diners feel uneasy.

"So I was thinking," continued the Rabbi, "maybe we could go sightseeing."

"Sure," I said, "where did you have in mind?"

"Well... I was thinking it might be nice to get out of LA for a while. Maybe go to Miami for a few days. Get some sun, sand and Sangria. All on me of course. Maybe we could make a couple of other stops too."

"Like a road trip?" I asked.

"Yeah. But by plane. First class. Whad'ya say? Come on, say yes. It'll be just like the old days!"

"Sounds like an idea," I said, thinking about it for a moment.

"I would love to come with you boys," Bella chimed in. "But my cousin's coming in from Norco tomorrow."

"Damn, that sucks. Two's company, but three's always better!" said the Rabbi.

"Yeah," I added, "what he said."

"Mom's always complaining about how she doesn't get to spend enough time with the sprog. I'm sure she wouldn't mind watching him for a couple of days."

"Speaking of your son, don't you have to pick him up

soon?" asked Bella.

"Damn, you're right. We should get a move on. We'll pick up the little man then I'll call my travel agent and make the arrangements for our trip."

4. Where The Mammoths Live...
A Safari Through An American Jungle...

Rabbi Glassman and I arrived in Miami as dawn broke across the state of Florida. I could take the risk of travelling by plane when I had my spiritual advisor with me. No-one would risk fucking with God in this bible-bashing, Mormon-hating country. Even the average coke fiend has to have some faith in the big guy in the sky while rolling up his dollar bill to inhale the white stuff. "In God We Trust". There was never any real separation between church and state. America's secularism was simply a convenient cover for military campaigns into foreign territories; sometimes for black gold, mostly for money. Countless wars had been declared against invisible enemies whose very existence was, at best, debatable. In the cold war they fought the 'evil' communists; many of whom were just taking a stand against the rapid cancer-like growth of capitalism. Then came the 'War on Drugs', targeting the young who were calling for the collapse of old establishments in favour of individual awareness. That battlefront was easily taken when the tools for perceived enlightenment eventually became the very means of mental and physical imprisonment. But this new millennium had brought with it a new threat: terrorism. It was the turn of the Islamic world to brace itself for vilification, along with anyone else who was a voice of descent. Airports were the front lines of defence in this crusade.

We checked into the Wyndham Gardens, a modernised and trendy hotel in South Beach that catered to happy holiday makers. But it also appealed to high class hookers and their johns; booked in for a few fun moments of unabashed pleasure. Women in these parts were generally looser than old screen porch doors and got banged with similar frequency. This was a place where a drink bought for the right woman could get you blown. Two might get her friend in on the action, and a twenty stuffed down her bra would buy you a quick fuck in the powder room. My associate and I had already been offered a sample eight-ball by the man in the next room. We didn't decline. There was more cocaine on these streets than in the entire film reel of Scarface. That stain on global cinema screens sparked a slew of copycat dealers. Every insignificant worm saw himself as the next Tony Montana, clad in a silk shirt and a cheesy suit to boot. Virtually all of them ended up behind bars, trying desperately to avoid being anally gang-raped in the communal showers.

There was now a resolute and dire need for a proper mode of transportation. We wanted to *explore*, see things the typical tourist doesn't get to; or perhaps doesn't want to. Most visitors get sold on the idea of the cellophane packaged vacation plan, sucking them into a getaway that's 'fun for all the family!' This was no way to get the true feel of a holiday hotspot. I was on my fourth visit to this cesspool of decadence and I was loving every minute of it. Most of the people who lived in Miami would up sticks in a heartbeat if given the chance; and I could understand why. Being surrounded by wickedness day in, day out is enough to give anyone a huge fuck-off ulcer. But my own character was so horrendously flawed that I thrived on monumental acts of misbehaviour. If the doctors had gotten their way, I would probably have been castrated during early childhood and put on a diet of Ritalin to numb my overactive mind.

We rented a Ford Mustang from the Avis people at the desk in the lobby; but we had to promise not to crash into pedestrians at high speeds. Initially, they asked us for our credit card information. I couldn't oblige as I was classed as 'persona non grata' with most rental, credit and insurance agencies. Over the years, I had been responsible for the destruction of one Dodge

Durango, a Ford Probe and a Fiat Coupe; the last of which met its end thanks to several spare canisters of kerosene, stored (for no particular purpose) in the boot of the bugger. The police in Glasgow were not amused by that incident. When they asked why I did it, I told them candidly "The fuckin' thing wouldn't start." They'd reported me to every authority in the region. I was sure that even Interpol were now keeping an eye on my every move. But the Rabbi, being a man of God, was able to assure the young lady attending to us that we were honourable and upstanding gentlemen; with honourable intentions. I suppressed the urge to regurgitate as I watched them flirt. It was a sickening display of ass-kissing niceness.

"Since you have impeccable credentials Mr Glassman, I don't think there will be a problem," she cooed.

"Thank you sweet child! God Bless your darling soul!" he said.

I watched her give him the keys. The old adage was true; the Lord certainly did work in mysterious ways.

By three o'clock that afternoon we were driving around Coral Gables searching for a bar I'd discovered on my last trip. There was no sign of it anywhere. And then came the terrible realisation that it had been replaced with a Denny's diner. There was nothing to be done, except to go in and sample the menu. To have quit and driven away would have been a waste of good gasoline. There was also the food factor to consider. My associate and I were hungry. The complimentary breakfast at the hotel had not been enough to satisfy our voracious appetites. But thankfully, extra large helpings of everything were the norm here. No plate on any table was left with a morsel on it. This helped explain the muffin tops we encountered on entering; a sight that should never be witnessed by a small child - or an adult lacking a strong stomach. Large women, who were otherwise attractive, chose to wear tight jeans and hot-pants, and the fat just poured out of their bulging waste lines, surrounding their upper thighs and sagging down, down toward the Earth's gravitational centre. Three years ago seeing a thing like that may have done something for me. In those years of mental disturbance I was experimenting with unconventional tastes. Now all it did was make me gag.

Fed and watered, we resumed our tour and ended up in Hialeah; this was not a part of town that Florida wanted to accept as being within its state borders. Although the entire city was crawling with Castro's prison rejects, this suburb was a snake-pit of degeneration. There was something about the street politic that created an excess of mayhem. Nowhere was it as evident as in the Walgreens car-park, where we stopped for aspirin and other assorted pharmaceutical compounds. There was a large four by four with spinning rims parked two spaces to our right. The reverberating bass beats echoed in its stereo speakers. The tinted windows rolled down and I was sure we were about to witness a daytime drive-by. The Rabbi and I hunkered down in case we got caught in the crossfire. But then, a voice growled and spoke in Spanglish.

"Hey mamacita, why don't you bring that hot little ass over to your papi! Come sit on my lap!"

The hyena behind the wheel cackled. The girl, who couldn't have been older than fifteen, looked visibly uncomfortable. We indulged in a spot of voyeurism and watched her as she adjusted her clothes and walked quickly across the street. Base animal behaviour. It never failed to shock; there was the amorphous face of evil. No actual crime had taken place, yet the look of humiliation and degradation in the young girl's eyes was unmistakable. The same was true of most rapes and murders. The perpetrators were innocent until proven guilty; but they were only guilty if there was no reasonable doubt; but no reasonable human being could be free of doubt; so they were innocent by default. Meanwhile, entire generations were being criminalised, shunned and rejected for wanting to explore bizarre ideals such as freedom, hope and love. People hooked on heroin, marijuana smokers and the mentally irregular were all harmful to the greater good. It was this twisted vision of social Darwinism that led many brilliant minds to live on the fringes, creating their own secret societies.

Suddenly, I heard the opening bars of 2Pac's California Love. The Rabbi took out his newfangled smart phone and answered the call.

"Rachel! Yeah, we just got into town... Actually we were on our way to the mall to watch the cattle in the bull-pen. We could stop by yours afterwards?"

He looked to me and I nodded.

"When are you free? Yeah, I know the address. Cool."

"Ask her if she's got any weed dude!"

"Oh, Max wants to know if... Yeah? Cool. Canadian eh? Cool. Ciao."

He turned to me as put the phone back in his trouser pocket.

"I wasn't sure if you wanted to talk to her."

"I probably shouldn't. Not on the phone anyway," I replied.

Rachel was great. The kind of woman with whom you could shoot the breeze, without the fear of the conversation turning to pink lipstick and hair extensions. Unfortunately, she was also a sex addict. This posed a slight problem one particular evening in the spring of 2005 when the electricity went out in her apartment and we were left alone on an idle Friday night. I wondered if there would be that awkwardness in the air when I saw her again. There was also the strangeness of my present predicament to consider. Like Oscar Wilde, I too had a love that dared not speak its name. A felonious feline had clawed her way into my affections. Her cat nature had entranced me. But Kandy was wild and dangerous. What would be the consequences of caring for such a hormone-driven, power-mad hybrid? I was certain that the RSPCA wouldn't take too kindly to my manhandling that kind of creature. There would be an outcry. Such things were meant to run free in the forests of exploration.

We pulled into the Dolphin Mall car-park and I searched the glove compartment for a pair of military binoculars, which we'd brought with us in case we had to watch the action from behind enemy lines. This was not a place your ordinary shopping junkie could handle. The bargain basement sale signs and free snack testing booths were strategically positioned to catch the eye of hungry customers on the go; on the war-path to the next sale. Like F-18s, they could refuel in middle of all the action. They would not otherwise make it through their commerce crazed spending sprees. This was the DMZ, where they fought, tackled and bruised to show the might of their purchasing power. The sight brought us a twisted sense of joy. They were like caged zoo animals being let loose to tear apart their jungle opponents. Little did the fools realise that despite being given the designation of 'valued consumers', it was they themselves that were being consumed.

The sun got lower in the sky and the time came to see Rachel. Better to bite the bullet and not prolong the impending doom, I thought. My chronic insomnia and jet lag weren't helping my nervous disposition. I fiddled with the radio in the car, trying desperately to pick up some station that didn't have a play list full of bitches, pimps and ho's. I'd once heard it said that rap music was a form of poetry. John Keats probably turned in his grave on hearing that. In the days of Gill Scott Heron, that might have been true. Rap and poetry were indivisible and real to their roots in the good old days. But now it was driven by lesser imitations of Biggie Smalls and Jay-Z. Testosterone induced lyrics glamorised the thug life and young gun-totting troubadours were its victims.

We pulled up at seven eighty six, 16th North West Avenue and made our way to the front door. I was as nervous as an Alabama tick-hound at a bluegrass jamboree. Rachel answered the door. Her long blonde hair swished over her low cut top, contrasting the green material covering her buxom breasts.

"Hey guys, come on in. I was just making margaritas."

I gave a quick wave and smiled slightly before she grabbed me and squeezed herself against my short body. I was feeling light-headed and dizzy from the heat. Her perfume seeped into my senses and I recognised it instantly. Chanel twenty two; the last birthday gift I'd bought her.

The Rabbi brought in a crate of beer from the car and I helped him carry the rest inside. We'd stopped by a liquor store run by Peruvian immigrants and picked up two cases of Budweiser and three quarts of Sangria. Rachel poured out the contents from her blender and the three of us sat silently on the couch and sampled the bowl of nacho chips next to the super-sized jar of dip.

It was only once we'd gone through two bags of Canadian grass, six beers, three margaritas and six capsules of Diphenhydramine that we felt truly comfortable. Just like old times. It was then that we were struck with the notion of going for a swim in the neighbour's pool; but before I stripped down, my associate pulled me aside. He was uncharacteristically drunk and it was obvious that he was not himself.

"She's fuckin' beautiful! I must have her! Bathe her and bring her to my temple. The spirit of God demands it! No, better yet, I'll lick her clean!"

There was certainly some kind of spirit going through him;

but it wasn't coming from any divine source. I tried to explain to him that it was unwise to let himself be tempted by a creature of lust. He was having none of it. In the end, I agreed to give them privacy for their pending 'religious' experience. It did make sense in the long run. If the Rabbi was the victim of her sultry charms, I'd be off the hook, Rachel would get laid, and the Rabbi would have an opportunity to spread his seed as well as his word. I went back into the house and rummaged through the Rabbi's jacket. Jackpot. Car keys in hand, I rushed out to the Mustang parked on the sidewalk. Darkness had finally descended, though a sticky warmth still clung to the night air. I turned the key in the ignition and the engine grumbled before settling into a slow hum. I drove through the Cuban district and coasted around the Miami Orange Bowl stadium, home to the Miami Dolphins for their first twenty-one seasons. Their greatest quarterback, Dan Marino, was a living legend and all-round American hero. But he'd retired in 1999. The Orange Bowl became pretty much defunct in that same fateful year when the Sun Life stadium became the primary host to pro and college football games. For an American Football nut like me, it was a bittersweet sight to see.

The all-night bars and clubs were beginning to open their doors to the long suffering masses, all standing in an orderly line; waiting for Lucifer to claim their souls. For a city that gave the lowest circle of hell a run for its money, it was surprisingly unassuming. The wasteland of human indecency was invisible to the naked eye; hidden in plain sight; paraded out every so often to entertain and shock the squares.

The regular Joe, with his Peggy Sue in tow, would never be caught dead in these avenues and alleyways. They would be busying themselves in gift shops with cheap souvenirs promoting Disneyland and the many fine Mom and Pop stores that were springing up on hill tops and highways stretching from coast to coast.

Hussies were flashing their breasts at every passing motorist and half-cocked client. The American prostitute is in a class of her own. She doesn't take shit from anyone and will not tolerate being called a slut until *after* she's seen the green. If you're short of the necessary legal tender, she'll hiss her tag-line at you as you roll down your window: "If you ain't got no money, take your broke ass home!"

I wasn't prepared to take any risks; not even for the finest blowjob this side of Kansas. I cruised on, past the redhead with the big round butt, and onwards, toward the beach. I could see the sand, lit up with lanterns and decorated with fire-eating circus freaks. Volleyball players dressed in skimpy bikinis and jogging shorts littered the seafront, grunting in the midnight hours while the moonlight reflected off their tanned silhouettes. I stopped the car in an empty parking bay and set off to join in the fun. The bronzed beauty sitting on the teak patio of the Seaside Bar waved me over and I found myself enjoying a cool Mojito with her while she talked to me about humpback whales and their mating rituals. She told me she was a marine biologist. We swam in the ocean for a while and looked up at the moon.

"Have you ever made love under the stars?" she asked.

"Can't say I have. There's too much smog in Scotland's cities to see them."

"Would you like to?"

"Sure."

She went down on me and we screwed for what seemed like an unending eternity while the waves washed over us on the shoreline. I was a horny toad in heat. The exhilaration didn't last long. In all the furore of impassioned fucking, specks of sand had crawled into my ass-crack and it was beginning to itch. We washed ourselves off in the warm water and went back to the bar for another round of cocktails and tacos. Spanish songs of love and loss pulsated from two damaged and badly wired speakers on the promenade. Mixed up feelings and confused memories surfaced in my intoxicated mind. I'd left Rachel's to avoid adding to my burgeoning bag of complex emotional problems, yet here I was, embroiled in another kettle of strange fish; out of the frying pan and straight into the napalm.

I paid for the food and drinks and bid the dusky devil-woman farewell. She rubbed her cheek with her forefinger and smiled as I got up to leave. I felt guilty for leaving her there like that, but it would have been foolish to take the situation any further. I didn't know her from Eve. She could have been an axe-murdering escapee from the local lunatic asylum. I quickened my pace as this thought lingered in my mind.

By 4am I was safely back in room 314 at the hotel. The maid had left fresh bars of soap and toiletries in the bathroom. I placed a call to room-service and ordered a Philly cheese-steak and another bottle of Bourbon. Twenty minutes later there was a knock at the door and a tall Cuban in a bow-tie entered carrying a plastic tray. I tipped him modestly and got down to the business of eating.

At 6am I heard someone fiddling with the electronic key-card mechanism. The door burst open and there stood the Rabbi, seething with anger, his teeth dripping with saliva, almost frothing at the mouth.

"Where the fuck did you get to?" he shouted. "Do you have any idea what that... woman did to me?"

"I thought you two were hitting it off. Besides, you told me to scamper, so I did."

"I expected you to come back with the fucking car!" he continued. "She wouldn't let me leave. That... bitch was insatiable! Five times! Five fucking times! I had to call a cab once

I was sure she was asleep!"

"I don't know what you're complaining about," I replied. "Sounds like you had a great time."

He wrapped himself in the bed-sheets and rocked himself to sleep, mumbling something about the nature of the beast. I was too tired to give a fuck. But I kept one eye open in case he felt the urge to tear my innards apart. We had two more nights to spend in this town and it would have been a shame to have our stay cut short because of my untimely death.

5. An American Werewolf & A Scotsman...
The Naked Truth & The Final Day In Miami...

Our three days in Miami culminated in a singular night of hedonistic devastation. We'd used up most of our money in Club Azucare. It was an unusual place, well off the beaten track. This, it seemed, was where the weird and wonderful gathered. Every fetish freak in Florida; along with an array of transsexuals, pansexuals, heterosexuals and asexual amoeba; all assembled together in this salad bowl of the South. Black, white, gay or straight; race and gender just didn't matter. The only prerequisite in order to participate in the games was an open mind; open enough to let your brains fall out onto the floor while the grey matter leaked out from the back of your skull. I had no problem in this respect. As a Scotsman who'd found his salvation in head-shrinking therapies and mind altering substances, I was prepared for any eventuality. The Boy Scouts had been robbed of a real asset when I'd chosen to never join their legions; though they were many.

Thirty-six hours of no sleep and a lot of tequila had left me slightly psychotic. The Rabbi was on the dance floor, making a fool of himself and practicing his own bastardised version of 'the laying on of hands'. He too had no trouble in adjusting himself to this scene. I suspected that this was due to the influence of his early career; before he became a conduit of God. He was unique in that respect. Not many men would have given up the lifestyle he once had to pursue what he referred to as 'a calling'. In fact, most would have happily checked themselves into a hospital under the care of an excellent physician; if only to sample the free psychotropic drugs.

We'd met before his conversion. I was in Las Vegas at the time with another friend who was facing a serious crisis in his community, and he persuaded me to go along with him on that long drive from New York City. Just north of the Nevada desert was a small Navajo reservation where he'd been summoned by the elders of his tribe, to help resolve a legal land dispute. While there, they encouraged me to embark on a 'vision quest'. It was to be the first of several. The general idea of the thing is that after spending a few days buried in hot sand from the neck down; and not taking any food or water; one achieves harmony with the spirit world. This is mostly assumed to be an urban myth, told to the white man to amuse him. But I found - much to my own astonishment - that it was a real and liberating experience. However, after a week of rough living and being no closer to enlightenment, I decided that enough was enough and I checked into the Rio All-Suite Hotel & Casino in Vegas. I caught the Penn & Teller magic show, and tried my luck at the fruit machines. I'd been told that your best chances always lay in picking one that was closest to an entrance. My grand total from the evening's winnings was zero dollars and no cents.

I drowned my sorrows in a Martini glass. The waitress shot me a come hither look and an amorous encounter ensued in a cleaning closet. We were locked into a deadly game of out-fucking each other, with no end in sight. I carefully made my way out of that broom cupboard forty minutes later and was met by a well dressed gentleman in a tuxedo. He stood there clapping his hands and congratulating me.

"Dude," he exclaimed. "That was awesome! You clearly have a natural technique with the hotties!"

At first I was concerned that he might have been watching the escapade through some obscure make-shift peephole, indulging some perverse past-time in the city of sin. But I thought it best to believe that he was simply acknowledging my magnetic personality. He introduced himself. Avi Glassman; film producer.

I recognised his name from my addiction days; those were long and lonely nights. The man was a legend in certain circles and we found that we got along like red-necks at a bluegrass barn dance. Unbeknownst to me at the time, the AVN award ceremony (considered the Oscars of Adult Entertainment) was being held in Vegas on that day. That was the main reason my future associate was there; he was a keen student of all genres of cinematic endeavour and he had a fine eye for talent. He introduced me to three other ladies of his acquaintance and we spent the rest of the evening popping amyls and enjoying the pleasures of their company. By the end of the evening, I was satisfyingly assured that these women were extremely well versed in the art of biblical knowing.

Now here we were in Miami six years later. Much had changed. We had grown older and wiser. We had a better handle on things; at least that's what we told ourselves through secret moments of self-doubt. It was the only way to keep the inner dragon at bay. Ours were fire breathing souls, chained in their desire to fly forever high.

My associate excused himself and went to the men's room. By my reckoning, he was gone a good thirty minutes and, for a short while, I was concerned that he might have been accosted by a Bolivian drug cartel. He returned. But my relief quickly turned to dismay when I discovered that he had purchased something so peculiar, I was left lost for words. I stared at him for a good twenty-five seconds while he flapped his arms around a metal cage.

"A man outside the rest rooms sold it to me for five bucks!"

"Five bucks?" I enquired. "Did you even stop to think if we needed a parrot?"

"Sure," he replied solemnly. "We need it!"

"You're going to have to explain that one. I'm afraid I can't see the intrinsic value of your newly acquired winged warrior."

"Well," he began. "It's like this. See, we're two free, foolish and drunk individuals right?"

"Yeah."

"And this is not just a parrot. It's a talking parrot."

"I see."

"So we're like pirates on the open Somalian Seas! We need a mascot to hoist our colours!"

I was not convinced.

"Didn't it strike you as a little bit odd that a complete stranger randomly offered to sell you a creature of the Avian persuasion?" I asked.

"Not particularly," he said. "You remember when that contortionist chick you were dating sold you her hamster?"

"That was different," I explained.

It was closing time and we were asked to leave. The Rabbi carried the bird for a while before handing it off to me. I was in no condition drive, and certainly not on the wrong side of the road. I climbed into the right side of the car, threw the Rabbi our car keys and clutched our feathered friend as we sped through the dead end streets. The journey back to South Beach was bitter-sweet. Not only was it our last morning, but it was also likely to be my last trip to Miami. The economic mess was driving out the mad ones, the bad ones and the beautiful ones, bringing in unoriginal big suits with their big bonuses. They were the only ones left who could afford to keep throwing away good money after bad. It was their final desperate attempt at holding onto some measure of control. Those of us aspiring to be true originals always knew that 'control' was nothing more than a fool's illusion. They got their freaky kicks from having it; we got off on bringing down that man-made wall brick-by-brick. But this city was now lost.

Back in the suite at the Wyndham, the shadow of impending doom merged with our toasted heads, creating a terrifying mix of rage and dread. The talking parrot hadn't spoken at all in the time I'd been carrying it, which agitated the Rabbi. I set it down next to the mini bar. The Rabbi, irritated at having purchased the defective squawker, started banging on the sides of the cage.

"Talk to me you hideous bastard!"

There was nothing but silence and an incredibly unnerving calm came over the creature. It was studying *us*. I threw a towel over the cage to prevent it from learning too much.

We were then hit by an urge to create a new type of table tennis. I was still harbouring a deep-seated anger toward Raphael Nadal for losing in the Wimbledon final. It was an abysmal performance, unworthy of any talented sportsman. It was this, I think, that led to us using the fire axes in the hallway to create a fair and fun competition, where two sporting gentlemen like ourselves would be pitted against each other in a deadly game, full of real mortal danger. The rules were simple. There was no need for any cricket, basket or ping-pong balls. Whoever chopped both legs off the coffee table first would be crowned king-champion, and this certainly was the sport of kings. But I was easily defeated by a man who had God on his side. It seemed only a logical progression for this fine game to find another arena. Sadly, the sheet-rock walls did not survive intact. We knew then that the credit card the hotel had on file was destined to be charged incalculable and serious sums for the heavy damage we were inflicting. But we were too far gone to care. At eight o'clock that morning, we were fully packed and ready to leave for New Orleans; our next stop on my tour of old stomping grounds.

The only thing left on the to-do list was to hand the car back to the rental agency. My associate spoke to the same girl that saw to us when we arrived. I was left holding the parrot. The Rabbi had no problem taking care of the situation, despite the strange scratches on the driver's side. They looked like claw marks. How did they get there? Had some hell-hound attacked us last night? Was one of us a werewolf in sheep's-wool clothing? At any rate it didn't matter. She signed off on the paperwork.

"I want you to have my prized parrot as a token of my appreciation," said Avi.

He took the animal and gave it to the stunned but overjoyed girl. It glared at us with a look of evil intensity, *knowing* that we'd pawned it off on yet another unsuspecting soul.

We were soon in a taxi with our luggage, on the way to Miami International Airport. They were hardly likely to start a nation-wide manhunt for two Jewish gentlemen with violent tendencies, just because of a few small marks on an automobile and a somewhat untidy hotel room. And if they did? I had a British passport. The British consulate would intervene or send in the SAS to facilitate my release from prison. Unless I ended up in Guantanamo Bay or in the hands of the CIA; which was possible.

But we couldn't afford to think like that. We had to remain positive, stay focused on the road ahead. The prospect of going back to New Orleans was a little bit like returning to the scene of a perfect crime; there's a little voice tells you it's a bad idea - but you can't help swelling with joy every time you remember that brief moment you almost got away with it.

Mason, my old drinking buddy, would be there to welcome us with open arms and sharpened fangs. Mason Lorn was, and still is, renowned for his skills in creating permanent vampire teeth for goth kids, lost to the extreme edge of alternative culture. His own fangs, he told me, were present since birth. I often wondered if he was the spawn of Nosferatu. During the day, he sun-lighted as a graphic designer of the highest calibre.

'Vampyrism', I learned, was a proper religion in its own right.

It was Mason who'd acquainted me with the underground subculture of vampyrism and blood-letting running rampant in New York City. New York was a strange place to be in 2002. The aftermath of 9/11 left a big hole in the spirit of the entire city. We all found ourselves searching for some sense of meaning, scared shitless by the possibility of chemical or biological attack by some suicidal fuckwit looking for the door to paradise; all so he could surround himself with virgins in a mythical promised land that rivalled ancient Babylon. This was not an easy thing to get our heads around and we were all left confused by these kinds of abominations. Of course, no-one could predict we would set loose our righteous ire through an unstoppable war machine. But for a very brief moment, those of us who'd witnessed the tumbling towers were one; irrespective of religion, colour or creed.

For many, it was a time of deep grief and I personally looked to the world of the weird to find answers. And so started the search, the voyage of discovery, which led me to New Orleans and to Mason. But it was during his time in Manhattan that he showed me portals to places I never knew existed. The 'Vampyre' freak culture was loosely attached to the bondage, domination and sadomasochism (or BDSM) scene, and it blended elements of Gothic culture, spiritualism and folklore. At the top of this heap of weirdness was a man we called Father Christian; a long-haired lunatic in Jesus sandals. He had as many screws loose as a nut factory. But he was worshipped like a God in the cult-like circles of the strange, always travelling with an entourage of submissive slave girls. Admittedly, I was intrigued by his philosophies and we became fast friends. But on one eventful night, in a place called 'The Red Room', our association came to an abrupt end. It wasn't unusual to hear loud screams of pleasure or pain in those situations, but it was the cry of 'Help! Help! Rape!' that made me spill my Johnny Walker all over the stylish burgundy carpet. I rushed head first into Christian's private room, which was a major no-no for any initiate. A young woman was sobbing on the floor. She looked like a bruised up thanksgiving turkey that had been basted and mauled. I felt compelled to hold a pen knife to the evil bastard's balls and for reasons that don't need explaining, I was promptly ejected, beaten and barred from the whole scene. Mason felt responsible and this whole thing put a strain on our friendship for some months. But a bottle of Glenmorangie and introducing him to his present fiancé helped us both bury the hatchet, figuratively speaking.

New Orleans had always been one of my favourite haunts, especially the French Quarter. Hurricane Katrina had brought with it a destruction that not only led to the deaths of countless innocents, but also decimated the hopes and dreams of thousands. I was told that the chaos and panic that swept the streets was unparalleled in its viciousness. Shops were smashed in, cars were vandalised and women were raped and sodomised by passing thugs without a scrap of decency. Yet the spirit of those people was unbreakable. It was not unlike the spirit of most Glaswegians or Londoners. Perhaps that was why I felt a kinship with the people there. They were as tough as they came. Hard nuts to crack; but some did, and they were still picking up the pieces.

The Rabbi and I checked our luggage at the appropriate desk, passed through the pornographic body scanners and waited to board our plane. We occupied ourselves with unabashed ogling, but that became boring very quickly and we indulged in some idle conversation instead.

"Man this has been one whacked out vacation. I owe you."

"Don't be silly," he said. "I think in some ways, I needed this more than you did. It's not easy getting old."

"You're not that old."

"True. But I'm getting there. When you have a kid, it ages you beyond belief!"

"I guess. I wouldn't know. I've never given much thought to having any. I'd need the right woman for that."

"Yeah. So, what's it like being back in old US of A again?" he asked.

"It's a funny thing. I'm not sure if this makes much sense, but it's like going to see a house you used to live in."

"How so?" he asked.

"Well suppose you go back and find someone else living in it. And then find out that they've redecorated the whole thing. It's nice to get the smell and feel of it again, but you know it's changed too much for you to be able to move back in."

"Makes sense."

6. The Final Trumpet Blows On The Bayou…
The Last Refuge Of A Scurrilous Scoundrel…

We arrived in New Orleans at around 2pm. It occurred to me that I hadn't written more than two lines in the travel journal I'd intended on keeping. Most of my time thus far had been spent ticking off boxes on some subconscious to-do list, birthed in the dark recesses of my warped mind. I needed to buckle down and make a proper start on the thing, and maybe think about finding a proper job on my return to Scotland.

Without a consistent and guaranteed income, no man can support himself. There were things like food and rent to consider, and I was already three months behind on the latter. With the damage I'd inflicted on my flat in Glasgow, I knew the landlord wouldn't be hard-pressed to decide on a swift eviction. There wasn't a wall or door that hadn't experienced a frenzied attack with a knife, crossbow and occasionally an 18th Century Japanese samurai sword. I lost my deposit the very day I moved in. But right now, none of it seemed all that important. I was a million miles away from those troubles.

Mason greeted us at the Louis Armstrong New Orleans International Airport and we sped away from the great Satchmo in the sky in his beat-up cherry-red Chevy Nova convertible, zigzagging through the traffic toward Mason's house. Very little had changed since the last time I'd visited. It was comforting to know that while the rest of the world was tilting on its head, rolling down and falling over itself, there was one corner where things seemed to be going at their own steady pace. The French Quarter was bursting at the seams with an influx of tourists. The energy was amazing. It was like being plugged into a 900 volt mains socket. The current was surging through my every nerve ending. We arrived at 620 Philip Street. Jewel, Mason's fiancé, met us at the landing and offered to help us carry our luggage. The Rabbi and I politely declined. Despite our personal failings as morally bankrupt and depraved creatures, I was still a Scottish gentleman, and he a holy man from the city of angels.

Jewel was a remarkably voluptuous and beautiful girl. She was Vietnamese by birth, but had been adopted by an American family at a young age. To describe her early life as turbulent would have been an understatement. She resented her birth parents for having abandoned her. She had no memory of them, but she couldn't understand *why*. Was there something wrong with her? Had they known that she was... different? Unable to reconcile this within herself, she had a total psychotic break from reality and began to push the limits of consciousness to extremes, testing herself in numerous fucked up ways, racking up an uncounted number of heinous transgressions, just to see where the line was. The family that adopted her eventually gave up on her. Yet even though she had every reason to become cold, her heart was open and her soul was warm. A part of me had once been tempted to make a move on her, but that was long before she and Mason became an item. He told me of his feelings for her one night in the middle of a drunken brawl with four Irishmen, which was not the most opportune of times to do such a thing. But after learning of his feelings for her, I did what I could to bring them together and they hit it off like two peas from the same pod. It was the least I could do for a friend who'd stood by me; even when I ended up on top of the Brooklyn Bridge, ready to take a nose dive into the black water below. The six degrees of separation. Everyone in my social circle eventually met everyone else, usually at some party or other. It was at one of these, that the Rabbi got to know Mason. We became the three amigos, wondering the lonely freeways of manly endeavour. It felt good to have the troupe together again.

After settling in, the four of us headed down to St. Charles Avenue, where the infamous and historic Pontchartrain Hotel stood. I'd stayed in it without major incident some years back. Sadly, its doors were no longer open. Mason told me that they were converting it into a residence for the retired. We looked on, admiring the building; the result of hard labour and artistic inspiration. We hit Magazine Street next; a shopping hub of sorts, where consumerism still had a human form. Several antique shops were elegantly spaced amidst the clothing and grocery stores. There was a quiet dignity to be found here that was not found in most centralised cities.

The New Orleans Mint demanded a look-in. I'd unintentionally avoided it the last few times; mostly because it represented a sort of metaphorical birthplace of money, which I had always regarded as an evil that had to be tolerated. There was either too much of it or too little of it, which presented its own set of sorrows for the terminally poor.

The mint had once played a prominent part in the beginnings of America, helping it to rise from the ashes and rebuild the lives of so many after the civil war. In a way, the North was still fighting the South; it was a bit like Scotland and England. There were two distinct and separate cultures occupying the same space and time; growing, negotiating and trying to find an acceptable status-quo. And this building housed the memories of a very important place and time, harkening back to another era of hardship. But it was now a museum, showcasing rare coins and minting machinery. Unbeknownst to me, there was a jazz exhibit down below. This was where distinct and fresh sounds took root; where men like Bunk Johnson, Jim Robinson and George Lewis had learnt and plied their trade. And of course there was my personal jazz hero - Mr James Booker esquire; The Bayou Maharajah; The Piano Prince of New Orleans. For me personally, it was like going on a holy pilgrimage to Vatican City. This was the Mecca of musical genius.

We refuelled on soul-food and soda-pop at a nearby restaurant then toured the port afterwards. As anyone from these parts will tell you, there is only one proper way to look into the murky depths of the Mississippi River, and that's by sailing on the last authentic steamboat; the Natchez. We got four tickets and trundled onto the vessel.

On the deck of the riverboat, Mason was unusually quiet and agitated. I assumed it was because I'd insisted on drinking eight cups of coffee, which put me in a caffeine crazed state. I was horribly hungover, so it seemed the logical thing to do. But the side effect of this cure was that it made me very hyperactive, and I found myself talking at a speed that made Mario Andretti look like a pensioner on a kid's tricycle. I contemplated the potential number of Youtube hits for such a spectacle before asking him why he was troubled.

"It's Jewel," he replied, "she breeched the terms of her parole again and they're talking about putting her back inside."

At this point in the chronology, I think it's important mention that Jewel, like me, had a nasty habit of getting herself into (and most times out of) every kind of trouble that was out there. There aren't too many people left that are either deranged or insane enough to live the life of a true hell-raiser. But Jewel and I were different. We were the free range crazy, roaming the cruel fast-tracks of existence, constantly searching for new and better thrills. Like the fabled swamp monster that lived in the Honey Island wetlands, we answered to no-one, lived for no-one and would die for no-one. We were the parent-less children of a desperate society that needed us more than we needed it.

"Don't worry about it," I told Mason. "Unless she raped a state trooper with his flash-light, they won't pay much attention to a girl who's fractured the occasional law; even if she has committed multiple felonies."

The prison system was overburdened and couldn't put away every oddball and degenerate who broke the rules. My own personal experience had taught me this. But I was worried that a parole officer would not see it that way. They didn't give a damn about the whys and the whats. They were small fry with large chips on their shoulders, with a whole lot of power to boot. But they were more dangerous than any big fish with an atomic arsenal of legal knowledge. Some were notorious for demanding sexual favours in exchange for lenient treatment and I wondered if this was perhaps what was really troubling my friend.

"She loves you," I told him.

"I know," he said, sighing.

"Well, make sure you hire a good attorney just in case," I added.

"Yeah. We plan on doing that. You're probably right though. This whole fucking thing will blow over soon enough."

I wasn't sure if he was trying to reassure me or himself. Then a voice suddenly yelled.

"I'll pray and beseech the Lord to grant you freedom from these demon troublemakers!"

Other seafarers snapped their necks round, tutting and muttering at us, and looks of disapproval beamed out from their generic and conventional faces. But they quickly resumed their mundane activities.

The Rabbi's pronouncement made us all feel edgy. We knew that when he spoke, mystic transmissions to a force beyond our comprehension were taking place. None of us dared to question him. The man; though I'm not sure if he *was* just a man; had a way of making things happen. This made us all wonder if he, like Moses or Nostradamus, was a prophet here to herald in a new century. He certainly believed he was.

The Rabbi and Mason took one of the many guided tours around the boat. Jewel and I opted to stay behind and take in the sights. We watched on as the sun set slowly across the bright blue sky. The changing shades of orange and red painted on the canvas of reality. Jewel broke the silence.

"Max... There's something I've always wanted to ask you," said Jewel.

"Sure, ask away," I replied

"Well... It's... I was wondering... How come you never ever asked me out?"

I wasn't sure what to tell her. I'd never really thought about it before. Most of my life had been a never ending sequence of things that simply happened: what actually was, instead of what might have been. I was afraid of looking any deeper than that. Afraid that I might find something so broken inside that it could never be repaired.

"Well J, when you have one damaged soul that's smashed beyond repair, it's not such a great idea to put it in an ice bucket along with another one that's also cracked," I replied.

She clearly didn't like the answer. It was plain to see that I'd inadvertently upset her. It was the honest truth as I saw it. I felt an inclination to apologise, but seeing no fault in what I'd said, I refrained. Perhaps it was that bit about being cracked. I tried to dispel the rising tension.

"Mason's a great guy," I said. "You really lucked out in that prize draw! Not even the lottery guarantees that kind of jackpot.

"And I really wouldn't worry about the parole thing. It's nothing more than a fly in the soup."

She nodded and smiled as she saw Mason and the Rabbi make their way back. Mason was well and truly besotted with the design and structure of the glorified skiff. The Rabbi however, was unimpressed by the boat.

We disembarked after the cruising along the river and went back to the apartment for a quick change of clothes. Mason suggested checking out the local night-life and it didn't take much to persuade Avi and I to go along for the ride. By 10pm, we were suited and booted and it was time to find the weirdness that was Club 735.

Despite our obvious sense of style, we realised that we were the most under dressed people on Bourbon Street. The Steampunk generation had gained momentum and gaps were being bridged between Victorian Gothic, grunge, punk, goth and Emo. New styles were emerging from all over the place and here we were, already antiquated like the discarded bobbles on Magazine Street. But we soldiered on. We could show the young generation a thing or two. They still took their cues from us and we would readily oblige.

Deep in the heart of Club 735, DJ AfroDizzyAc's set was pumping out supersonic tunes that were splitting atoms in the atmosphere. The people at CERN didn't need that overblown Hadron Collider. Millions of tax-payers' dollars could have been saved if they'd spent an hour here.

In the middle of the dance hall, a jaw-dropping rope suspension and strip show had begun. The dexterity and skill required was astounding. The girl herself was a gorgeous blue haired beauty. I felt a stirring in my lions as I watched her take off her bra, twirl it around and throw it into the crowd. I was right at the front, next to the performing area. She winked at me, extending her forefinger and beckoning me to follow her with my eyes. At the end of the act, she flexed her calves and did the splits, and I felt an overwhelming desire to lick her stomach. Luckily, I was able to resist the temptation. The coolers were on the lookout for deviant behaviour and they didn't look kindly upon the exchange of precious bodily fluids in public.

I pushed my way through the mass of human flesh, until I got to the naked barmaid with heavy make-up and colourful full-body tattoos. I admired her artwork for a moment before I heard her speak.

"What is your pleasure, sir?"

I knew what my pleasure of choice was, but it was difficult to communicate it to this demon princess. I opted to stick to a list of beverages.

"Two Jack Daniels, one Bloody Mary and a Grasshopper," I replied.

I watched her trot off to the shelf where the bottled liquor was kept and admired her sweet posterior while she measured out the alcohol. She had two puppy dogs inked above each breast and on either side of the perfect cleft of her ass were two bluebirds. She returned carrying the order in her arms. My friends were all gathered at the far end of the club. It was going to be another night of hard drinking and sinking into moral oblivion; and it had just begun.

7. To Sleep, Perchance To Dream…
A Farewell To Outstretched Arms…

It was 4am when we made our way back our refuge. The streets were packed with revellers making their way back to their own abodes. I was still buzzing from the five bottles of Bud and eight Bacardi Breezers. A private jam session was taking place in my head. There's nothing more gratifying than having a great tune jangling in your head at morning o'clock after partying hard. Even endless hours of debauchery can't compare to the satisfaction that comes from the musical genius of certain artists.

My shirt stank of rum. I detected the smell of sex in the air. Mason and Jewel had been bumping body parts at some point earlier in the evening. My only bone of contention was that I'd missed out on all the action. I'd been too busy; engrossed in a conversation with a shaven headed, tattoo sporting barmaid. We'd been discussing the pros and cons of scrotal piercings. But I was rudely interrupted by the Rabbi half way into my argument.

"We've run out of beer money!" he screamed.

At first I was angry with him, but I understood all too well the seriousness of the situation. Without an adequate intake of alcohol, we would find ourselves waking to the chronic terror of reality. Had this happened in our early years, we would simply have killed ourselves and checked out of this godforsaken Earth life. But if it happened now, it would require something considerably more drastic. It was then that I remembered the secret stash of money I always kept pinned to my underwear, in case of emergencies. This qualified.

When I turned, the barmaid had disappeared and I was left clutching my rum with just the Rabbi for company. If only I'd acted on my earlier impulse to molest the stripper, I wouldn't have found myself alone with that damned song swirling in my head. I couldn't even remember who sang it.

I must have started singing aloud because the residents of Philip Street began hurling insults in our direction almost immediately. We stood there, swaying on the steps, as Mason searched through his pockets for the key to his front door. It was a tense moment. We all experienced the anxiety, feeling sure that we were one step away from having our mail redirected to a temporary space on the pavement. The New Orleans Police Department didn't look too kindly on the homeless. Thankfully, we were saved from being bludgeoned for vagrancy. Jewel reached into her purse and rattled the key-chain in her hands.

Inside, two uncomfortable single guest beds had been set up in the living room. I didn't understand why they'd gone to the trouble. They knew I was set to leave for Chicago in four short hours. Still, it was better get some rest before being subjected to the trauma of airport security again.

I had no intention of straying anywhere in the windy city. Were it not for the fact that I had to change flights at O'Hare to get back to Glasgow, I'd have avoided that entire wretched urban hell-hole. It was full of dullards and winos, and provided little in the way of excitement. Those kinds of quiet cities, run by mobsters and pimps, perplexed me. It didn't make sense to fill a place up with people, then watch them waste away. Each one counting the minutes until their next heroin laced hamburger fix.

The window was open. Stray dogs were fighting on the side-walk. Images danced around the walls as shadows flickered from the dim street lights. My brain slowly switched off and I dreamt of a girl who sliced up her heart to satisfy my hunger.

With morning came the rush to pack my belongings in some orderly fashion. I hadn't brought all that much to begin with; which should have made it easy. But the difficulty lay in trying to find my lucky cream coloured socks. I was wearing them when I arrived. I was certain of that and after forty-five minutes of searching, I discovered them in the garbage can. There was no time to put them in the washing machine, so I washed and rung them out in the bathroom sink while I showered. And thanks to Jewel's very expensive hairdryer they were instantly bone dry and ready to wear.

"MQB! Were you using my fucking hairdryer?" she scowled.

I couldn't tell her why I was using her personal high-grade appliance to dry a pair of $5 socks from Walmart. And there was no way that a bald man could get away with saying that he was borrowing it for personal grooming.

"No!" I shouted back. "Ah... That's just my electric razor... I'll be done in here in a minute!"

I heard her walk into the kitchen and turn on the percolator. I quickly put the hair-dryer back where I found it and quietly walked out. I was beginning to feel uneasy about going back.

"Om Mani Padme Hum." I recited this Buddhist mantra repeatedly as I put on my snake-skin shoes.

I'd spent several months at a Buddhist retreat in northern Scotland during one particularly horrendous phase of unrequited love. I don't know if it was the calming influence of the monks at the Samye Ling temple, or simply the fresh air that gave me a feeling of oneness; but I soon felt healed and unburdened. This feeling didn't last long however. One idle afternoon, I was discovered with a past issue of Playboy magazine featuring Pamela Anderson as the centrefold. That woman had plagued my early years with her broken promises of sweet suffocation. Her lips never moved; they didn't have to. Her eyes did all the talking that was necessary. After being deemed a bad influence on other lost truth-seekers I was politely asked to leave; which I did, thankful that I had gained a profound understanding of the cosmic order of things.

I fumbled for my passport and airline tickets. Passengers, like pilots, have to perform a series of pre-flight checks in order to maintain industry standards for cattle-class. And we paid dearly for the privilege of life in the age of air-travel. There were fuel taxes, airport taxes, landing taxes, carbon taxes, baggage taxes, travel insurance, life insurance, death insurance and of course ensured insurance. It was inevitable that some greedy bastard somewhere would come up with the idea of charging money for using the on-board lavatories. If you couldn't afford to pay, you would suffer the indignity of not making it to the toilet on time

With everything packed and ready, I folded up my guest bed. The Rabbi was set to leave for L.A. the following day. The four of us had breakfast at a small coffee house on Bourbon Street. We watched warm hues from the sun bounce off passing cars.

I ordered blueberry pancakes. Café Beignet was like something out of an Edward Hopper painting, serene and inviting, yet sombre.

"It's been a blast having you down MQB. Wish you were sticking around for a little longer," said Mason.

"It's been good being down man," I replied.

He nodded and smiled. His sharpened teeth sparkled. The Rabbi ate his omelette in silent contemplation. I could see from his pained expression that he was missing his son.

"You'll be back home tomorrow my friend," I said.

"Yeah. It's been great hanging with you guys," he said, "but I gotta tell ya, it'll be good to get back home. Hey Mason, how much would it cost to get them kinda teeth?"

Mason stood up and walked over to look at his teeth, hovering above him as if he were an dentist giving a proper consultation for a thousand dollars an hour. Jewel stretched out her hand and took mine as it lay flaccid on the table. She pressed it firmly and opened her mouth to speak, but no words came out.

The two men finished their discussion came to the conclusion that it would be too expensive and generally pointless for the Rabbi to even consider getting fangs.

"Well dude, we'd better get you to the airport," said Mason.

"Yeah, the clock is ticking I suppose, and they do say that you should ideally check in two hours before take-off," I replied.

He loaded my luggage into his car as I said a tearful goodbye to my friends. I bid farewell to the Rabbi and we shook hands and hugged. The car ride was short. Little was said by either of us. One question kept going through my mind, "Why are you leaving again?", "To go home." I told myself. Home. It seemed like such a strange word. Nowhere had really felt like 'home' in a long time.

We approached the designated unloading area for transatlantic air travellers. Mason and I thumped our chests as a sign of our enduring friendship. There was an unspoken bond between us as friends and as men. He popped open the trunk and I took out my bags before going into the terminal building. He waved and drove off into the distance. I looked at my watch. It was high-noon precisely.

Inside the terminal building, there was an extensively long queue of lost souls all waiting to be accepted into the bosom of a sardine can with wings. I was in no immediate rush to board, only to check in and make it through security. One angry traveller insisted on being upgraded to first class for free. When the manager refused, he lunged at him with his ball point pen. The customer, of course, was always right. I imagined that in their worst moments, the air crew had sick fantasies about decapitating passengers with starched pillows as they passed through the aisles offering tea, coffee and blankets. But for now they had to endure and smile sweetly at the hordes of venomous vertebrates.

Finally, my turn came.

"Hi, do you have your passport and ticket?"

The brunette woman behind the service counter seemed pleasant enough. I reached into my trouser pocket and gave her my travel documents along with a half broken polo mint.

"Please place your luggage on the belt."

I did as she asked. The steel weighing machine beeped and the display flashed with '15 Kg' in big red digits. There was a large whirring sound and suddenly my bags were gone, delivered into the hands of some half-witted handler who'd toss them around like it a bottle of cheap aftershave.

I bought the latest issue of the New York Times and flicked through the pages while I waited for my boarding number to be called. The biggest news on the front page was the president's plan to raise the debt ceiling; plans that were being stalled by the Republicans in the House of Representatives. What troubled me was the complete lack of foresight on the part of our fearless leaders. 'Oh, Obama you misguided fool! Surely you realise that raising the debt ceiling will only lead to a bigger mess.'

With no real financial growth since the recession, all he'd done was to secure his own term till 2012. Like Pontius Pilate, he'd leave America to the cruel tortures of the tea-bagging right-wing crazies.

The UK was virtually in the same boat. I suspected that even two generations down the line, there would be little in the way of change. The rich always got richer and the poor got nothing for their troubles except a stamping from the size 10 shoes of some Tory, Liberal or Labour peer with a duck pond;

who of course needed our charitable donations to keep it clean enough to wash his dirty laundry in; away from prying public eyes.

The East African famine barely got a mention on page eight. Those horrific images we'd all seen on our TV screens during the eighties hadn't made a damned bit of difference. Governments were still selling arms to ruthless dictators in exchange for their blood money. Meanwhile, earthquakes were rocking nuclear reactors in Japan, economies across the world were on the verge of collapse and innocent children were starving in places with unpronounceable names. And there wasn't a fucking thing Bob Geldof could do about it.

The loud speaker sounded off and broke my train of thought. "This is Continental Flight sixty-three from Louis Armstrong New Orleans International to Chicago O'Hare which will shortly be ready for departure.

I was seated next to a hockey fan wearing an Anaheim Ducks t-shirt and I felt sure that meant trouble. But I got to Chicago alive and well. The pressure was mounting and I started to feel nervous. There were only thirty minutes before the gate closed for my connecting flight to Glasgow.

I ran to the gate with ten minutes to spare and arrived to hear my boarding call. Once the metal bird was in the air I breathed a sigh of relief. The first few hours were spent looking at the little monitor in the headrest in front of me. I was in right in the middle of taking down critical readings when a female voice broke my concentration. This was no time to be disturbed by idle gibber jabber; Distance travelled, ETA to destination, and our present position. These were essential things to know if we went down and needed to radio for help. But what if we went down in the ocean? Who would find us then? There would be no chance of our surviving that kind of appalling situation. Giant sting rays would barb us to death and lobsters at the bottom of the seabed would swallow our tongues.

"Sir, can I get you anything? You seem a little... unsettled," said stewardess.

I turned around and my saucer like eyes met with hers.

"No. I'm perfectly fine. Just a frequent flier on holiday. But tell me, can you serve drinks yet?"

8. Glasgow Smiles Better...
The Prozac Fairy Makes A House-call...

Thud! The landing gear hit the tarmac with all the grace of a Welsh rugby player doing the tango. My ears had popped whilst we'd been in the air so I made moose calls to rebalance the pressure. It took a while before I could hear properly.

The other travellers all scuttled and screeched like feral monkeys. I gathered my thoughts and waited patiently for them to leave before getting up. Immigration wasn't going to be a problem. I was just a Scotsman returning to the dear green place. All I had to do was state my name and flight number.

I walked to the baggage reclaim area and casually lifted my case off the conveyor belt. A customs officer walked towards me.

"Oh shit! Not again!"

"Sir, could you walk this way please?"

"Could you open your suitcase? We'd like to examine it."

Every portion of the suitcase was thoroughly poked and prodded and searched through. Another shorter man joined in the fun and brought what looked like a miniature vacuum cleaner to the party.

"We've detected trace amounts of cocaine with your belongings," he said.

"Cocaine?" I mumbled, "I don't understand. I don't know what you're talking about!"

"There's no need to get worked up sir, It's too small an amount to be of concern to us. Where are you flying in from?"

"New Orleans," I told him.

"Ah. Someone probably passed you money used in the consumption of a class A drug. Those bloody Americans do love their drugs! Be careful in future. You're clear to leave."

A mixture of shock and joy bubbled up inside me, but the happy feeling soon subsided when I realised there would be no-one to meet me here. I got into a large white Volvo with a 'Renfrew Taxis' sign on the roof. Volvos were reputed to be the safest cars ever made.

Fifteen minutes later I was at home. I took a deep breath and unlocked the front door. A sea of junk mail crunched under my feet. Some promised cash prizes of a hundred thousand pounds, others offered cover for the over fifties. I didn't qualify for either.

I opened some of the letters and paced around, praying that one might contain a cheque I was owed for work. Most were reminders for unpaid bills, some going as far back as May. I threw them into the abyss of the kitchen trash can. If they wanted the money bad enough, they'd remind me again same bat time, same bat channel.

I glanced at my calendar and opened more of my mail. Bingo! There was a cheque. I'd inked something on the Sports Illustrated Swimsuit Calendar. It was a note to remind me. A local author had the bizarre idea of standing in the middle of Buchanan Street to read his latest novel aloud from start to finish and had invited people to watch. Aloysius Drummond was one of those strange people whose creative spark attracted a vast array of interesting characters. Women were especially susceptible to his brand of intelligent madness. It would be interesting to witness, if only for my own sick amusement.

I thought it best to get some shut eye before catching this public spectacle of self-flagellation. I picked up my mobile phone. Kandy had been in my thoughts a lot. I decided to send her a text in the hope that she'd agree to come over.

"Hi. Back from vacation. Feeling supercharged. Can you come over?"

The phone beeped with a message alert.

"Glad ur back. Did you have a good vacation? Was in London myself for a few days. Yes. I can come over for a bit after work."

I tapped out a reply on the keypad.

"Had a great time. Hope you had a good time in London. Will see you later."

Beep.

"Will come down around 8.30. K."

At one o'clock I was rudely awakened by the noise of a beer barrel delivery at the Old Govan Arms. My head was pounding with an extreme pain; akin to a thousand rodents dancing and clawing their way through my frontal lobe. I got up and flicked open the blinds.

"Keep it the fuck down out there! Decent people are trying to sleep!"

They men across the road shrugged and carried on. That was the Govan way. People often spoke of the poverty and deprivation that existed in these old tenements. Though it was superficially true, it lacked real perspective. We looked out for each other. While money-rich city kids and third generation immigrants lived off the fat of their parent's income; buying fancy cars, and condominiums; *we* were busy building bridges to the real future. Treat your neighbour as you do yourself. A long-haired hipster preached the same thing once.

Drummond would still be reading to jakeys and panhandlers; inadvertently educating them and raping their minds simultaneously while they heckled and spat glue-like sputum in his direction. It seemed too enjoyable a sight to miss and I had that cheque to cash anyway.

I took the bus. It passed near Elder Park. New soulless brick homes were going up where the world famous shipyards once stood. There was a certain sense of sadness in seeing so much change so fast. The whole area seemed a little darker.

It was a short walk to Buchanan Street. The revamped House of Frazer seemed emptier than usual. So did most of the other stores. The usually busy Argyle Arcade was faring no better, despite being home to numerous jewellery stores. The last time I was in there, I saw a diamond ring, selling for the princely sum of fifty thousand pounds.

"That's nothing," said the Jeweller, "last week we sold a bracelet for a hundred and twenty thousand pounds."

Who were their customers, I wondered. No Glaswegian of my acquaintance had that sort of cash.

I stopped by the Cheque Centre. The man behind the plastic window counted out the money and handed it to me through the metal drawer. He smiled at me and it made him look like Hannibal Lecter.

Outside, I saw Drummond a few feet from the old Tardis-like blue police call box. It was now an ice-cream vending station. Crouching on the ground, at his feet, was a bevy of beauties, staring longingly at his six-foot three-inch frame. I remembered that I'd seen something similar in New York.

The man had the luck of the gods. No questionable junkie types were in sight. There was no humour to be enjoyed at his expense. This harmonious scene must have come about because of his choice of clothing. He was smart. His dark Mafia suit screamed 'Fuck with me at your peril! I'll slice you into tiny pieces and stuff you in a deep freezer!' I assumed the lotus position on the ground and rolled up a cigarette, listening carefully to his punchy prose style.

J. Daniel Solomon was also there. He was a gifted writer who'd spent his thirties years living in an Israeli kibbutz. In an earlier life he'd been a practising lawyer. I'd never bothered to ask why he left the profession, but I assumed it had something to do with the gritty realities of crime, or seedy divorce cases revolving around midget sex maniacs and animal prostitution rings. He agreed that it took a certain level of psychosis to attempt something like this. Who else but a Glaswegian would think of doing something this disturbing; inviting public ridicule instead of avoiding it?

"... I thought you were in America? When did you get back?" said Daniel.

"I was. I got back this morning. How've you been? How was your trip to France?"

"It was very nice. I managed to get a start on my third book," he said.

"Is it a follow-up to the last one? You might end up like George Lucas and his Star Wars saga if you're not careful!"

"Yeah. It's a follow up. But it's more along the lines of another book I read, which focused in the inter-personal relationships between middle-aged men," he said.

"Sounds heavy... but good," I replied.

Boredom eventually overtook me. There was a small photography shop in Merchant City, which I often wandered into on days when I could afford to. My interest in cameras began at the age of ten when my grandfather bought his very first Minolta. The family appointed him 'chief photographer' at every occasion.

My father followed this up one year by urging everyone to pitch in so he could rent a video camera. We all got a kick out of that. We'd gone for months living on boiled rice, but when the behemoth sized thing arrived one afternoon, it didn't seem to matter. We all took turns being BBC cameramen reporting on the Beirut conflict. My grandfather also had a fondness for practical jokes, and the fact that he could get them on tape pushed his inventiveness to new levels. There were banana skins, empty tea cups, and buckets of water placed above doorways. My father did not appreciate that at all and frequently blew up like a mushroom cloud of radioactive anger. I inherited my grandfather's twisted sense of humour as well as his flair for photography, but also embedded somewhere in my genetic code was my father's violent temperament.

On the second shelf in the window at £300 was a 17-85mm zoom lens that would fit perfectly onto my Canon 500D. I stepped inside and saw Jack the manager standing behind the counter.

"Max! Good to see you young man! What can I do for you today?"

"The Canon 17-85. Can you put it aside for me? I'll be back for it next week."

"I can do better than that my friend. Since you've been a loyal customer, I could give it to you on credit."

On credit? What was he thinking? Obviously he didn't know about my general habits regarding previous possessions that were also bought on credit. When I say bought, I mean never paid for.

Jack removed the lens from display and wrapped it in cloth and bubble-wrap.

"Do you need a carrier bag?" he asked

"Yes, I think so. It might rain later on."

I headed to St. Enoch Square Underground. Glasgow's subway system was second to none. It was one of the most effective means of public transportation. Kelvinhall – my stop. I went by foot to the Art Gallery and Museum. It boasted one of the largest art collections in the world, with numerous paintings by well known artists. They had rules about food and drink that were punishable by testicular electrocution, but I smuggled in a can of Miller I'd bought at a nearby snack store.

By seven pm I had seen everything. I walked home. Sauchiehall Street, near Kelvingrove Park. That was where I saw the shameful sight of a badger flagrantly masturbating in a public place. It was the sort of thing that just wasn't acceptable in family friendly locations. I thought about reasoning with it. I wondered if it had the capability to understand. Did it get off on knowing that people were watching? Would it able to comprehend the word 'wrong'? Perhaps it was best to leave it be. But it's a sorry state of affairs in our good country when things like this happen and people just walk on by: a true affront to our sensible Christian values. I bought a newspaper from a street vendor and tucked it under my arm, aiming to catch-up on the latest goings on in the dry safety of my house.

I spent a few moments reading the headlines. Rupert Murdoch, the Australian/American tycoon, had been implicated in the phone hacking scandal.

I'd heard brief whispers about it during my trip. I knew that he'd taken a beating like a red-headed step-child on the Wall Street stock-markets, but I hadn't really understood the root cause behind the whole thing. Some members of the Metropolitan Police had been in league with crime-happy journalists, illegally hacking into the phones of private citizens; allegedly; all for the sake of selling more newspapers. A parliamentary committee was set up to investigate and they summoned the mighty Rupert and his bastard progeny. The slippery fucker had effectively refused to respond to any of the questions put to him, feigning memory loss - "I know nothing," he said.

But the leading news story on the front page of every newspaper that day wasn't about his fiendish plans for world domination, or his media empires horrendous practices. Instead, the focus was on an angry member of the public who'd thrown a custard pie at Murdoch Senior. A gnawing animal was digging its way out from the pit of my stomach. How much more of this cheap bullshit could we be expected to take from that stupid skin stealing freak? He already had influence on what we watched on TV and who we should vote for on Election Day. It was his corporation under Fox News that had declared the 2001 presidential election in favour of George W. Bush in the US. Who gave a fuck if he had a paper plate of shaving foam thrown at him? If there were such a thing as real justice, he would be decomposing in the innards of a giant squid. There was also the matter of the flesh hanging from his decaying corpse. No ordinary human being had that much excess skin just hanging from their face. The only possible explanation was that he had been stealing the skin of unknown victims during a demonic sex ritual involving a headless kangaroo, a succubus and the Red Chinese.

The buzzer rang and broke my train of thought. I peeped through the keyhole. It was Kandy. She was early.

Kandy was 'petite'. She stood at five-four with brown curls and a small waist. I presumed her hair was dyed because I'd seen a hint of blonde in her roots once. Her green eyes reflected innocence. Behind them was a razor-sharp brain of lethal cunning and terminal intensity. I sensed an edgy energy while she stared at me like a predator with a mind to kill. She strode into the kitchen and asked for one of my cigarettes. She was the epitome of a femme-fatal right out of some dime-store noir novel.

The atmosphere was tense. We chatted for a while. She asked about my vacation and I quizzed her about London. That was when the vibe turned nasty.

"It wasn't great. Last time I flew down with my friend Linda. This time I went by coach, which was a bad idea. I stayed with my ex. We fucked like rabbits, breaking up and making up."

I felt my blood begin to boil and it rose, unstoppably upwards, searing my temples.

'Calm down,' I told myself, 'maintain control… There's no need to let the situation get unpleasant. Om Mani Padme Hum.'

She asked me to read her some of the work I'd done on the travel journal. I obliged, trying to maintain a Zen like state.

"You're an amazingly talented writer," she said.

She began to sensuously stroke the plant sitting on my window sill.

"Don't you touch my plant!" I yelled

She seemed stunned by my reaction.

"I should go," she said.

"That's probably a good idea," I replied.

She struggled with the sticky lock, trying desperately to escape the ugliness of the situation. I held her quickly, hoping that the pure emotion of love might quell the torrential downpour of negativity. It did some good, but the damage had been done. I spent the rest of that evening slashing through my newspaper with a flick-knife in the vain hope that the deepening jealousy and anger would expel themselves from my core.

The following day seemed no better. Despair crept in and joined forces with malicious feelings of hate. There was but one course of action left open to me. I picked up the phone and dialled the pre-programmed number.

"Good morning, Dr Miller's surgery. How can I help?"

"I'd like the first appointment you've got please," I croaked.

"I've got one space at 9.30 am."

"Yes. That will do very nicely," I replied.

I dragged myself out of bed and made myself presentable. The clinic was relatively empty bar two other patients who had their eyes fixed on the screen overhead, spouting good health and well-being sermons, all sponsored by one drug company or another.

"I'm here for my 9.30."

"Take a seat. The doctor will be with you shortly," replied the receptionist.

After a few minutes a droopy eyed old fat man came out and called me into his office. There were three chairs opposite his and I couldn't decide which to take. I paced around the room nervously.

"Well, I'm heart-broken, depressed and spent yesterday evening having fantasies about disembowelling Rupert Murdoch," I said.

"Interesting," he said, clicking on his computerised prescription pad.

The printer whizzed. He leapt to his feet and thrust a piece of paper into my hands.

"Get this filled in our pharmacy at once! As your doctor, I'm recommending sixty milligrams of Fluoxetine - Prozac - twice daily. More if you need it!"

9. The Scales Of Two Cities…
Lust & Lamentation Make The World Go Round…

I tried to maintain balance as I made my way to the bathroom. My legs felt like jelly. I could hear music playing in the background. I'd left the CD player on repeat through the night. 'Unchained Melody' rang out in all its glorious agony while I evacuated my bowels. I flushed the toilet and washed my hands with coconut fresh anti-bacterial soap. My bloodshot eyes glared in the bathroom mirror; the redness scorching the wall behind. I was endlessly drifting through an ethereal mist, sedated on prescription pills, bottles of bourbon and piss poor 80's pop music. My fragile mind had been fractured by pervading morbidity. There I was, ripped up, hyped up and doped up; forced to conform in the opium den of emotional angst.

I slid the panel on the medicine cabinet and picked up a small carton. 'Warning, May cause drowsiness. Take only as directed'. No shit. I popped three pellets from the packet inside.

I walked into the living room and switched on the television. The sight of a fifty-inch news anchor greeted me. He was interviewing a spokesman for a well known right wing party. The man had a great deal to say on the ever present issue of immigration and 'the great Muslim debate'.

"Radical Muslims are taking over this country! They want to implement Sharia law in all of England. We can't let other people dictate our way of life. We are British and we must be proud to be British!" he bawled.

His concept of nationalism brought with it images of a half-crazed Adolf running around the gothic cities of Germany. It was odd that a rational human being; part of an overwhelming ninety-five percent majority; would feel threatened by a mere one percent of the population. But I did understand the fear. Some didn't feel their voices were being heard by the all mighty institutions designed to represent them. It was only natural that they would descend to the level of stupid apes, seeking someone to blame in a perverse hysteria. The enemy within. The media relished it.

The phone rang. I didn't want to speak to anyone. It rang again and didn't stop.

"What!" I yelled, ready to smash the handset off the wall.

"Jesus, Max! It's James. I was just calling to tell you that there's a Syrian poets gathering tonight at the Centre for Contemporary Arts. Thought you might be interested in coming along."

"Jimmy, I'm not really feeling too hot right now. Doubt I'll be there. When does it start?"

"Tomorrow at eight. If you can make it along, it'd be great to see you there. These guys went to a lot of trouble to get here." He hung up.

I looked up at the pendulum wall clock. It was already two-thirty. The overcast sky made it even less appealing.

The condition in Syria was getting worse. President Al-Assad's crackdown on his own people had resulted in the death of innocent civilians. These poets had taken a big risk in travelling thousands of miles to come to Scotland; all so they could share their art and plight. It seemed only good manners to go four miles to see them.

The situation with Kandy was still troubling me. I didn't like the way things we'd left things. I called my friend Elayna in Liverpool. She would no doubt have some wise words on how to restore karmic order and universal harmony.

"Eli? Hey! It's Max!"

"Max! Nice to hear your dulcet tones! Are you back from your trip state side?"

"Aye, I got back yesterday. Eli, I was hoping you could offer your usual sound advice on something that's running circles round my brain."

She listened carefully as I told her about the truck-load of problems I was having. She muttered something about scones and the lack of them south of the border. I rolled up a cigarette and flipped open my Zippo lighter, waiting for her sage response as my thumb rested on the flint wheel.

"You're a fuckin' idiot," she said. "Why did you handle it so badly?"

"I got jealous and angry," I said.

"You need to apologise quick-style if you want to make things right."

"Me? Why? Hey, I wasn't in the wrong here!"

"Yes you were!" she insisted. "You should call her right after you put the phone down and grovel. This isn't the fucking '50's Maxwell. Things have changed."

"What the fuck are you talking about woman? Don't you think I know that? But let's be honest here a second. I'm an alpha male. I hate the subjugation of woman, but I'm not inclined, or built, to grovel. Besides I can't call her. It'd be too bloody awkward."

She thought for a moment and I could almost hear the gears ticking in her mind.

"...Fine. Don't grovel. You're such a moron! I'll tell you what to do. Write her one of those wonderfully honest letters that you're so good at writing. After all, that's why we're still friends isn't it? Well that and your tyrannosaurus like stamina. You were always the one that got away," she said, with a flicker of regret.

I was a left a little red and embarrassed by her comment. Back in the day, we weren't exactly friends and we weren't exactly lovers. We'd been something in between that never quite gelled. It was always a case of wrong time, right location; or right time, wrong place.

"Cheers ears. I knew I could count on you. I'll send you some scones and a case of single malt. Ciao baby-doll."

I mulled over what she said. Perhaps Eli was right. There was no real harm in sending Kandy a letter, if only to set things right. I swung open a desk drawer and took out a piece of paper and rummaged around in search of a decent pen.

"Dear K,

I've chosen to write this letter to try and explain my recent actions and behaviour. A conversation with a friend today made me realise that I'd acted like a child throwing a rattle out of the pram.

I don't think it was wrong of me to be a little miffed. Clearly, there were things that had been building up in what Jung what have called my shadow side. But it was wrong of me to let this darkness permeate into our communications.

There are some ailments for which God grants us no cures. Things that vex us in our troubled moments. Sores that tear through soft flesh, and memories that haunt u; fierce terrors that burn into blackness.

I'll clarify that last part for you. Contrary to popular belief, I'm not Superman. I am, in fact, a man. And as a man, I'm imperfect. I carry scars from the past and you already know about the heart-stabbing pain I suffered at the hands of Selena.

I do care for you very much. But with you not knowing what you want in life and love, it doesn't make for a stable friendship or relationship of any kind.

You're the harmony in my soul. I've never met anyone quite as captivating.

Love on ya, M."

I considered whether I should actually mail the thing. No, best to do it. One less thing to worry about.

I poured myself a small glass of bourbon and took a swig to clear my scattered mind. With my frustrations finally down on paper, I felt a sense of relief. Maybe it was the medication. Maybe it was the bourbon. Either way, it didn't matter.

I thought about all the times I'd spent in Kandy's company. It was then that I realised I was prepared to take her good, her bad and her worst, which was a first for me. I wondered how many other men were sitting in their comfortable chairs thinking the same thought, feeling the same feelings, for her.

10. The Ballad Of A Kandy Coated Toffee Apple...

She lay on the bed next to me wearing a pair of baggy pyjamas and my black talent scout t-shirt, exhausted from the emotionally draining few weeks she'd been through. Nothing sexual happened. We just lay there, peacefully, staring at the ceiling, talking about our respective dreams for the future. Hers revolved around fame and fortune. Mine were simpler; to keep breaking rules until I grew old or killed myself in some spectacular fashion.

We'd spent the evening in my flat, watching DVD's and drinking hallucinogenic teas imported from the Himalayas. I kissed her during the directors commentary, but she stood there, quiet and stiff as a board. I figured maybe I'd gotten my wires crossed and decided to call it a night. She was too tired and too high to make her way home safely at three o'clock in the morning. I offered her the option of taking the bed while I would sleep on the couch.

"No," she said. "You don't have to do that. I don't mind sleeping next to someone."

"Okay," I said, "but I warn you. I sleep like an eleven stone baby. Don't be surprised if you hear me burping, farting and snoring through the night."

She laughed.

"That's disgusting!" she said.

I smiled at her and gave her a quick peck on the cheek before closing my eyes and lowering my head onto the duck-feathered pillow. I was beginning to nod off when an angelic and gentle voice suddenly said

"...Do you want to see my breasts?"

This doe-eyed twenty-something old had caught me completely by surprise. What was the appropriate response? Yes?

No? Phone a friend?

"Of course," I said as I reached over to kiss her again.

Her lips were soft and sweet. She took off the t-shirt and covered her nipples with her hands, nervously smiling in a sleepy haze. Her hands dropped to her side and her milky white skin glowed in the mild light of the scented candle by the window.

Things were heating up. She gazed blankly at the floor.

"I can't do this," she said.

"You don't have to do anything you don't want to," I told her.

I held her close for a few moments and we both drifted off. A few hours later, I was woken from a deep sleep, realising that she was grinding against me uncontrollably. Naturally, I responded in kind.

"I want you inside me! I want you to fuck me hard!" she whispered, breathless from the dry humping.

Night passed into day and I got up to replenish precious bodily fluids while she slept. I prepared a smorgasbord of various treats for breakfast, including fresh blueberries. She'd told me once that they were her favourite. I quickly popped down to the florist around the corner to buy her fresh flowers as a parting gift, in case I never saw her again. Kandy was about as unpredictable as they came. No-one had ever figured her out; which made her interesting.

When she came out of the shower, I sensed that things were already different. The weather was warm but her aura was cold. She sat quietly munching the crunchy marmalade toast and scooping up blueberries by the handful. I lit a cigarette and inhaled the smoke deep into my lungs, hoping that the toxic fumes would kill me before the conversation became awkward.

"I have to go soon," she said, "I have to meet someone who might put my band on the map."

Kandy was an indie generation rock chick who'd grown up with the cheap factory produced music of the 80's. It eventually bored her and she found herself drawn to the underground club beat scene, with hardcore rhythms and hardened disc-spinners. Her life revolved around fast base lines and faster living; a succession of quick fucks and fumbles in search of some unknown.

I'd met her purely by accident. They say bad things happen in threes: maybe it's true. That same day, I'd gotten into a fight with a freakishly strong homeless woman who proceeded to steal my chrome toaster. That should have told me something, but I didn't realise that in the same evening, I would find myself attracted to a hot-stepping crazy girl. She was performing at the Victoria Bar, with the passion of a wildebeest in heat. I couldn't contain my enthusiasm and immediately after the show I introduced myself. We sized each other up in the equivalent of a scorpion mating dance.

As I got to know her better, she told me things about her past. Things that filled me with rage and anger. A history of sexual abuse had turned an already troubled child into a hell-raiser of epic proportions. She ran into the arms of every gruesome son-of-a-bitch she had the misfortune to meet. For a lot of them, Kandy was simply their fuck toy, a dirty little secret, a fetish they indulged in to satisfy their needs. I became the latest in a long line of no good bums. I had no pity for her. She wasn't a victim; not as an adult. But I did have all the love in the world for a girl who wrestled with her demons daily. It took its toll.

To see an otherwise intelligent woman go through moments of extreme suffering pained me greatly. In Islam the notion of Jihad is often spoken about – the struggle. From my own experience, I knew the toughest wars to fight were the ones we fought within. Hopelessness sets in and the devil you know comes calling to collect his dues. It seems strange that we live in an age when we can wipe each other out with Uranium smart bombs, but there's nothing that heals the wounds inflicted on the spirit of another human being.

Kandy's spirit had been broken and remoulded in two parts. Psychiatrists called it bi-polar disorder. They say it has to do with genetic predispositions, or overwhelming circumstances. Whatever name they gave it, whatever reason they gave for it manifesting, there was no actual cure. There were however, plenty of drugs produced by pharmaceutical companies to reduce or manage the symptoms. Kandy didn't believe in using drugs; legal or illegal; it didn't matter to her. She once railed at me for what she called my excess use of medication.

"You're no good for me," she'd said. "You're too much of a chemical freak!"

Perhaps she was right. She was heavily into alternative therapies, and I had nothing but disdain for them. All I'd seen in the new-age miracle market were charlatans looking to make a quick buck; or fake messiahs showing the way to the kool-aid. I was all for philosophic ideologies that challenged the system; religious or economic; but few, if any, had altruistic reasons for propagating their newfangled quackery. Usually some insider blew the whistle on whatever angle they were playing and the whole house of cards came tumbling down.

I sometimes wondered if Kandy and I were little more than fuck buddies. We didn't even qualify as friends to fall into the 'friends with benefits' category. What added to the confusion was that I was not the only rooster in the hen house. Most women realised that their power lay in being able to limit who got access to their souls and beds. Kandy was not so discerning. It occurred to me on more than one occasion that maybe she got her rocks off watching men fight over her in a jealous heat of primal passion.

Did that make her sick? Not in my eyes. She was a product of her environment. If she was seen as sick, then it was a reflection on those that saw her that way. She had the kindness and compassion of the Dalai Lama in the best of times, and it was this that I found to be her most attractive quality. These traits were rare to find in anyone, and I certainly didn't have them, or need them. I envied those who did.

Kandy's main release wasn't sex or even booze, but rock 'n' roll. Writing songs and singing till her heart bled brought her a sense of peace. It was her confessional, where she communed with her spirit guides. A way for her to reconcile the truths that conflicted within, bringing together that half of herself that she could barely face with the one that gave her the strength and resilience to carry on day to day.

I didn't see or hear from her again for over a month. I assumed that she'd keep herself amused with her other 'interests'. When she finally did call again, I found that my suspicions were correct. But the green-eyed monster showed no signs of appearing. I figured since we didn't have any kind of defined relationship, there was no justification for allowing those kinds of feelings to surface. I had no idea how quickly that would change.

"Hey Kandy, How you been kid?"

"Hi Max. I'm good. New job's going well. I got that position as a support worker! I told you about it remember?"

I couldn't remember.

"Got a glowing report from my boss too! Want to read it? I'll email it to you."

"Sure, send it over. Kandy, I got to see you again babe. I'm missing you like crazy."

I'd been pushing myself to the limits with odd jobs and an equally intense nightlife, leaving almost no time for social activities. I had a fire in my nuts and I had to do something to relieve the stress. I wanted her. I needed her.

"Well, I would love to see you, but I'm pretty busy. We could meet tonight... let's say around 9.30. There's something else you should know. Robbie came down and spent the weekend."

Her voice sounded strained. Was it worry? Fear of my reaction? Perverse excitement?

"I see," I replied.

"Are you mad?" she asked.

"No, I'm not mad."

"Oh," she sighed, sounding almost disappointed.

"I'll see you tonight at 9.30."

I showed up at half past nine on the dot as we'd agreed and knocked with my usual four knocks. She seemed surprised when she answered the door. I'd never been late, so I wasn't sure why. She invited me in and we embraced quickly before I made my way to the Ikea couch in the middle of her living room. I'd walked there from a small tea-house nearby on Pollockshaws Road. There was no question that I was out of shape. I hadn't renewed my gym membership in months and that may have been part of the problem. I wiped the sweat off my brow as she walked into the kitchen.

"Do you want a cuppa?" she shouted.

"Yes, thanks, that would be great."

She set down two mugs on bourgeois coasters, filled with very weak tea. It was how she liked it. I didn't understand the point of going to all that trouble of making tea, only to sip on what amounted to water and milk. Kandy made herself comfortable beside me and we talked about her work and issues that were plaguing her life. I didn't have much to share because of the daily sense of sameness that was ever present.

"My feet are killing me!" she said.

"Would you like a foot rub? Some say I have magic

fingers, as you might know."

I gave her a cheeky smile and she moved her feet up to my lap. I massaged her left foot gently as she lay back quietly, closing her eyes. My pulse began racing when I moved onto her right foot. She pulled up her skirt past her knees and rubbed her thighs. My hands made their way upwards, cupping her calves. She had sensuously long and sexy legs and she knew I was getting more turned on by the second.

"Are you hard?" she said.

"Hard as a rock," I replied.

Her lips met mine and we kissed gently before I felt her supple breasts against my chest. We made out in what seemed like a perfect moment, frozen forever in eternity. Her hand reached down to my belt buckle and she bucked as I my crotch rubbed against hers. It wasn't long before my jeans hit the floor and the sound of buttons popping echoed through the room. Then, out of nowhere came the words.

"I love you Kandy."

I kissed her neckline, while in the back of my mind, my subconscious was mulling over the implications of the last moment. 'What the fuck did you just say?' it asked, 'Are you fucking crazy? ...Don't tell this girl you love her! ... She's dangerous! You're insane!'

It was two am. Kandy looked up at me as I cradled her in my arms, her hand in mine. She broke away and had the same distance in her eyes that I'd seen the last time. She got up and paced nervously through the apartment, clearing up bits of clutter, packing away boxes of make-up and accessories. I'd once read in a medical journal that obsessive compulsive disorder sometimes also affected people who were bi-polar, especially when the sufferer became overwhelmed with conflicting emotions.

"You should go soon," she said. "I have to be up early

tomorrow and..."

"You don't have to explain," I told her.

I held her close again and placed a kiss on her forehead.

"I meant what I said earlier. I love you."

"I... love you too," she said, as her lip quivered slightly.

I left and made my way toward the main road, hoping that I'd be lucky enough to catch a taxi. It was a warm night, and I was prepared to walk all the way back to Govan. Luckily, my hunch paid off and I saw the glimmer of an amber taxi sign rushing down in my direction. I flagged it and got in.

By the time I got back to my flat, I was feeling uncertain and on edge. I'd left the lights to prevent intruders from breaking in and stealing my plant along with my beloved Barry Manilow LP collection. I picked up the phone and placed a call to my old friend and spiritual advisor in Los Angeles.

"Rabbi? It's Max. I'm feeling fucked up and a little lost. I wasn't sure where else to turn."

"Hey buddy. Long time no speak. What's up meshugana?"

"It's that girl. I don't know what the fuck to do. I really like her, but my head is all over the place."

"Listen dude, You gotta get her out of your mind. This girl, she ain't no good for you. You listen to Avi now. I'm telling you, don't let this fester. Put her out of your mind and out of your life. Shalom."

11. A Cultural Cataclysm in a Dear Green Place

It was another wet Wednesday night. It hadn't stopped raining since the day before. The weather forecast had predicted exotic temperatures and more sunshine than Aruba. They may as well have hired voodoo shaman priests to do bone readings. They'd have had a better accuracy rate. It seemed silly to expect a tropical climate in a country that experienced long winters colder than Siberia. Last year, all of London ground to a complete standstill following an inch of snowfall. I recalled how we in Scotland had laughed at the time, proud of the fact that we were tougher, made of sterner stuff. It was only when we got record amounts of the tiny white flakes, that we took the problem seriously. That was when we stood shoulder to shoulder with our English counterparts, the same stiff upper-lipped, Londoners who we'd mocked as weaklings just weeks earlier.

I filled the bathtub with hot water and weird bath salts and spent the better part of an hour playing with my rubber duck in the foamy bath gel. I was sorely tempted to stay cocooned in the comfort of the tub. I'd taken an emotional battering and was in no mood to go to the Syrian Poets convention. Not many folk were likely to be there anyway. But I knew I had to dig deep and find the strength to attend. My gut told me that it would be worthwhile, and experience had taught me that it was always better to satisfy curiosity than to be left pondering the possibilities. One of Gerry Anderson's puppet shows had put it best. As a kid, every Saturday morning I snuck into the lounge to tune the damaged fourteen inch black and white TV, just to hear that booming introduction, 'Anything can happen in the next half hour!... Stingray!"

But it wasn't the action that interested me as much as the intricate personalities of the characters. People had always been my drug of choice. It was safe to say that I was a social addict. The good, bad and the ugly all caused different reactions in my distressed mind. Fabulously mad optimists with hints of intelligent delusion were like uppers, inducing highs that lasted for days, weeks and sometimes even months. They were the artistic oddballs that bought into the gimmick of false confidence and endless hope. Spending time with the sad and solitary, however, quickly counters those magic moments of mania. Downers: too many of them and you bought yourself a one-way ticket to Introspection Bay and Gloom Central.

What kind of people I was likely to encounter at this gathering? Were these foreigners prone to the same strange tendencies as us civilised westerners? They were a curious breed of desert people, willing to speak their minds on what they thought and felt. This, said their religious scholars, made them a force of evil. They were corrupting the youth with their notions of self-expression. It was all the fault of the decadent infidels. Perhaps he was right. We certainly weren't in any position to judge. Our own society was falling apart before our very eyes. 'Broken Britain' - that was the buzzword concocted by our government to describe it; as if at some point it had been perfect and then been trampled on like a toy train. To fix it, our freedoms had to be taken away. It was for our own good. We needed it. It was not, of course, in any way similar to the Arab Spring situation.

I got out of the bath and put on a clean pair of boxer shorts. Still feeling lethargic, I closed my eyes and took a deep breath. There was a half empty bottle of Southern Comfort sitting on the kitchen worktop. I reached into the rickety cupboard above to take out a whiskey glass and filled it with ice. I've never understood people who drink anything neat, unless it's a single malt. All liquor, especially blended scotch, always tastes better on the rocks. My formative years in high school had been spent drinking warm bottles of Buckfast behind garbage sheds and I'd grown to dislike the forced necessity of forgoing ice-cubes on warm summer days.

The hour was fast approaching. I stuffed a compact Kodak camera in the inside pocket of my black biker jacket. It was too late to take the bus but I had just enough time to call the cab company and get there by taxi. It was never a good idea to show up at any event after the first thirty minutes. The spotlight typically ended up on the latecomer who, after clanging the doors shut, would almost knowingly step on the toes of seated spectators for a brief, twisted thrill. You could always hear the groaning from the irritated crowds. They'd all mastered the art of pre-planning, which naturally made them better than any shambles of a writer.

'Fuck 'em,' I thought.

The car arrived promptly. I ran out and jumped into the back of the cab, instructing the driver to take me to Sauchiehall Street. The pressure was mounting and I could feel the adrenalin coursing through my veins. This was the boost I needed. I began to look forward to an evening of obscure poetry that I wouldn't understand.

"Step on it!" I said to the man behind the wheel. "Come on man! Is this a car or a horse driven cart?"

"It's a Skoda," he replied. "It can do about a hundred if I push it. But this is a main road and the limits thirty."

"Speed limits are made to be broken," I said, "besides, they're more like suggestions."

He didn't seem amused. "Do you want to get out and walk? I can let you out here if you want to be a dick about it."

"No, no. This is fine. Just get me there in your own slow-ass time."

He pulled up to the kerb after a tense ride.

"That's six pound and fifty."

I paid him and stepped onto the pavement. He drove off, gave me the finger and sped away. I turned my attention to the bright lights in the town centre. There was something almost hypnotic about Glasgow at night. I stood there, right outside the entrance to the Centre for Contemporary Arts. A large colourful banner hung from a lamppost, waving in the wind, welcoming street walkers and students alike into the bosom of culture. Its doors were the golden gates of this Emerald City.

There, standing in the foyer, was Jim, scanning the stairs for familiar faces. He was smartly dressed in his sports coat, jumper and jeans. A blue raincoat was bundled in his arms. I approached him and held out my hand, ready for his usual firm handshake. Instead, he flung his arms around me and patted me on the back. I was a little shaken. He was a slender man, but his six foot frame gave him an advantage over most. His ever growing auburn hair had become fluffed and frizzy from the windy conditions.

"Maxwell! It's bloody good tae see you! How've you been, dood."

Jim was one of Paisley's finest poets and a communist sympathiser with connections to worn out faces in dangerous places. In Hoover's era, he would have been bundled into the back of a van, never to be seen again. He'd fought staunchly against Thatcher's poll tax in the '90's. Those were tough times. Times of mass unemployment, yob culture and deep despair. The whole of society had gone back to the 60's, hoping to find some nugget of wisdom. But all they got was a promiscuous, heroin induced orgy of fucking and being fucked over. The youth spawned from the soup of free love found that nothing, not even love, was free. Forced to face this fact, they turned to the arts as a means of escaping the horrible realities of today.

As well as being a champion of an age long gone, Jim was also a rip-roaring drunk; the only man I knew who could drink me under the table. He had the constitution of a bull and the libido of an African rhino. It was obvious he was inebriated. Although not entirely sober myself, I wasn't noticeably intoxicated. Jim's present condition, however, was easily guessed when he moved toward a slim, freckled redhead wearing glasses and told her that she had shapely legs. His observation couldn't be faulted. She didn't respond and showed no immediate reaction. Jim stood there bemused. The girl turned toward me.

"Your friend is incredibly rude!" she said, slapping me across the face.

She grunted and left with her nose upturned. I was completely dumb-struck. Most women usually responded well to compliments. But it was Jim who'd come onto her, not me. I was thoroughly confused. My cheek suddenly felt hot and began to sting.

"We should probably head to the convention. Where are they doing this thing?" I asked.

"The Studio Room, I think. Aye, we should go now. That was strange. Very strange indeed," he said. "Oh I've pre-booked seats for us so there's no problem."

The two of us thought about what had just happened as we ascended up the stairs and into the main entrance of the Studio Room. I reached for the door handle and paused.

"What exactly did you say to her, Jim?"

"I just told her that my friend and I thought she had beautiful legs."

"Oh," I said.

"And then I asked her if she had a sister and that I'd pay good money to see them get off with each other."

"Ah," I said. "That would have done it."

On opening the door, we discovered the room was packed and that the show had already started. We hurdled over the seated audience and clambered into the empty chairs with 'reserved' tickets placed on them. Jim fit in perfectly with the rest of the crowd. They were all well-turned out in their Sunday best.

I, on the other hand, looked like a common thug who'd barged in unannounced to gatecrash the event. The only other patron wearing a leather jacket was the inimitable Alvin Biscuit. But his was tailored-to-fit in the form of a suit jacket. There was a gold chain hanging from his waistcoat. He was the only soul I'd met who had a functioning fob watch, and he used it for all practical purposes. He abhorred the internet and the slack-jawed generation who swore by it religiously. Although he was well under forty, he took his style tips from Winston Churchill. In his spare time he was a Scottish nationalist who advocated independence for Scotland. This made him a fun sight to watch in debates against royalists. His better half, Christine McMannus, was sitting beside him in the back row. Alvin was a renowned novelist at the forefront of contemporary Scottish writing, while Christine was well known for her numerous short stories, which had been published in every literary journal this side of the grave.

In front of us, a short, stout young man with a dark complexion spoke feverishly into a microphone in his native tongue. I could barely see him and I certainly couldn't understand him. This made the whole performance difficult to follow. The wooden pulpit hid his face, with only his forehead remaining visible, glistening from the overhead lights as beads of sweat trickled downwards. When he finished, a tall blonde woman from the first row stood up and glided onto the podium.

"Thank you very much Ali Ibn Yousef, for that moving piece. I'll now read you a translation in English....

The spring wells in Arabian eyes.
The water burns into oil, into blood.
I cry, I cry.
For my mother, for my father.
My tears run clear.
Dying under the midnight stars.
Dining on ashes in sand and dust.
Lights burning dimly,
Fires dancing in the night sky,
Spirits of the righteous crushed.

Diamonds in the desert,
Hearts yearning for truth,
Beating against the bombs.
Give us life, let us laugh.
Love! Free us from your hands.

Shackle our souls,
Our goal is one,
Dropping mortars of mind.
We are peaceful warriors,
Walking with the angels."

A small ripple of applause built up into a loud wave of unending appreciation. The young man whose poem had just been interpreted stumbled slightly as both he and the translator stepped down.

Several more readers took to the podium, but none had the elegance of the first. That may have been down to their own interpreters. I wished I had the ability to understand the language. Never before had I felt so sorely lacking in knowledge.

By the end of it all, several members of the audience rushed the stage. It was like a rock concert, only with less noise and considerably more droll. What got my attention was the fact that these people had escaped persecution to share their life and word. They were real people with real problems, unlike me; a self-involved idiot suffering from the self-inflicted pain of a broken heart. Some of them had danced with bullets to make it to the ballot box.

Jim and I quickly exited the room and made our way to the bar next door. The drinks were anything but cheap. We spent the better part of an hour nursing our Corona's, planning our next move. There were plenty of clubs and pubs around, but few appealed to our tastes. Most were little more than glorified fuck pits; catering to student troglodytes, who crawled, climbed and drooled over each other to reach the prettiest girls. For refined drinkers like us, this was a pointless exercise. We waited for the girls to come to us. Of course, it was a flawed plan. There was a plethora of fish in the sea, but rarely did we cast our lines in the right oceans. Normally we got stung by jellyfish.

Then it hit us. The Griffin. One of the finest drinking establishments we'd had the pleasure of frequenting. And so it came to pass that we staggered toward the legendary boozer. There followed several unconnected conversations about Robert Tannahill, Romany gypsies and the importance of pinning your wallet to your underwear as a theft prevention mechanism.

"How dae yae feel aboot Rasputin?" asked Jim.

"Rasputin?... You mean that crazy mad Russian fella with a fetish for flagellation?"

"Aye, him!"

"Kinky fucker wasn't he? Do you think he got it on with the Queen?"

"He must've done Max. There's no way a sex mad Russian

priest would have turned her down."

"Yeah, you're right enough. Still, at least he wasn't part of the priest mob today, what with all the bastard buggery of young kids and that. Those fuckers make me sick. I'd shoot each one of them given the chance!"

We'd been walking for some time down Sauchiehall Street, and I began to question whether we were even going the right direction. When drunk, my inner compass; both moral and geographical; became utterly useless. We came upon Elmbank Street. I was ready to cross the road and carry on walking, but Jim grabbed my arm and pulled me around the corner.

"Where are you going Max? It's doon this way!"

About half a block down, we saw the bright lights above the sign. The nectar of the gods was sure to flow freely in the infamous saloon. I imagined that heaven, if there was such a place, wouldn't be entirely dissimilar: a pub with a custom built lounge and free cable TV featuring one hundred dedicated sports channels. We stood silently for a moment, adjusting our eyes to the halogen lamps before swaggering in like John Wayne and Paul Newman.

12. Australians Don't Give A Four X...
A Mythical Maestro Makes An Appearance...

An indiscernible rabble of voices greeted us inside. The mild tones of soft rock blended with the sound of a thousand conversations. Sitting on a barstool in the far corner was Evan Mackleson, a successful screenwriter and serial novelist. With him, Roger Van Winkleton, a poet, painter and patron of the arts. I'd never met the man, but his thick moustache and horn-rimmed glasses had become the stuff of legend among the bohemian art community. I signalled Jim to join them. The barman glared at me like a Doberman ready to pounce on his unsuspecting prey.

"What'll yae have?" he growled.

"A pint of Guinness and a Speckled hen," I retorted, squinting slightly.

He could see that I was not a man to be trifled with and threw a white dishcloth over his shoulder to signal his surrender. In the arena of pub life, each pint pulled was a deadly game of chicken. Every barman was a potential friend or foe. The wrong choice of poison could result in sudden death, or a slow form of social suicide.

Jim hadn't moved. He was still fixed to the same spot next to the door, his eyes glazed over and he adopted a thinking man's pose.

"Max, whit does that look like tae you?" he asked.

"What does what look like?"

"There, up there, next to the men's room."

"That? Well, that's obviously a big fuck off stain. Probably from damp or a leak or something."

"Look closer. Seriously, just look at it," he said.

I did as he asked. It took me a while to register. He was right. There was something emerging from the pattern. An image started to take form. There was no mistaking it. There he was; a bearded man with long hair emerging from the piss and water stains above the gent's restroom.

"Jesus!" I said

"Aye," said Jim.

"Man, that's freaky. That's better than that Turin toast on e-bay."

"No kiddin'. Come on son, we'd better join them two over there before they start wondering why we're staring at the men's toilets."

"Yeah. I only came over to tell you to move your ass; not to stare at trippy religious iconography in a leaky pub."

In the artist's corner, both men got up and greeted us. Evan was a short, round-faced man with ginger hair and a Che Guevara styled beard. A true revolutionary. He believed in the power of the people. Some called him a mad reverse futurist, others saw him as a genius. According to him, modern society was doomed to decay and everything would soon revert back to Dickensian times, with workhouses and prisons. Technology would meet its demise and the tide would turn, rolling back through the years until nothing remained.

I didn't share his bleak vision. If anything *was* going to destroy us, it would be our emotions. Those were things to which no-one was immune. No ancient bird god or long-haired desert preacher could save us from ourselves and our ability to hate. But I was hopeful. Evolution had spared us so far and the process itself might one day lead to the elimination of all our irrational fears.

I drank my pint of Guinness as Jim and Evan tried to discuss Marxist philosophy in coherent sentences. I was already past the point of comprehension and only chimed in every so often with an "interesting", or "I see", to avoid seeming out of place. Roger was busy staring at a girl with pigtails. I could understand why. Her muscular thighs wrapped in a miniskirt left nothing to the imagination.

"So Max... What do you think about this whole free market capitalism thing?" asked Evan

"Eh, well... I guess..."

"Hey Evan, check out the rack on that cute number!" said Roger

I was glad for the distraction. It took the attention off my brain-dead responses.

"Oh she's got it going on awright. But the missus would kill me if she knew I was perving!"

"Don't be daft," I said. "What she doesn't know won't kill her."

"That's true. But she's meeting me in here in ten minutes," he replied.

"Well, unlucky you," said Jim, "I'm gonna have a crack at her. Nothin' tae stop me lads!"

We watched with anticipation as Jim got up and charged towards the young brunette. She seemed unimpressed and her body language became defensive as he thrust himself into her personal space. It was obvious to everyone but Jim that she was becoming more disinterested by the minute. Ordinarily, when he wasn't quite so drunk, women found him to be charming and amusing. But his decency took a back seat when he'd had a few.

"Get away from me you dirty old man!" screamed the girl.

Jim came back to the corner, sulking like a misbehaved child who'd been caught by the teacher.

"Maxwell," he said, "It's entirely possible I'm a wee bit drunk."

The three of us cracked up, unable to stop laughing. At first, Jim didn't see the funny side of it, but it was infectious and he soon found himself chuckling with the rest of us.

"I guess it's my round," I said.

Evan suddenly became very still and his face lost all expression.

"I've just seen Jason Donovan walk through that door," he said.

"Who the fuck is Jason Donovan?" asked Roger.

"Jason Donovan?" I said. "Are you sure? What the fuck would Jason Donovan be doing in Glasgow? "

"I'm sure man. It was him. But I could be wrong. We should double check. He's just gone into the lounge."

We all looked at each other with a look of confusion. None of us wanted to meet the man and we weren't quite sure whether the old rule of backing up a friend applied in this situation.

"Come on guys, it's Jason Donovan! He used to be one of Australia's biggest soap stars!"

"I still have no idea who the fuck Jason Donovan is!" said Roger.

"Oh come on guys. Please," said Evan, "he knows Kylie!"

"Oh!" we replied.

"He might have her number," he added.

"Well... I've had a crush on Kylie ever since I can remember," I replied. "This girl I was stuck on; she kind of looked like her."

The others still seemed unsure, but I wasn't going to let them stop a potential romance dead in its tracks. I got up and followed Evan toward the saloon.

"Listen man, if he doesn't give us the information we need, I say we hit him over the head, tie him up and drag him across town till he spills the beans!"

"Max, I don't want to kill him, I just want to meet him."

"Who said anything about killing him? Just a little mild

torture."

"Torture? No, I'm not going to torture one of Australia's best exports for some bint's phone number."

"Fuck you man! You take that back!" I said sternly. "Kylie is not a bint. She's a goddess! Perfection personified! A true vision of beauty!"

"Okay Romeo, take it easy. Let's just find the guy first."

There he was, sitting alone at his table with a 'Sound of Music' script in his hands and a pint of Australian beer beside him. That's when it hit me. It was the reason he was here. I'd read in some tabloid rag that he was set to star in the musical at a local theatre, though I couldn't remember which. We hovered nearby, looking for an opportunity to present itself. That script was our ticket in, for Evan to meet one of his twisted heroes, and mine to possibly meet the pop princess of my dreams. His glass was empty before long, and we spotted our chance to go in for the kill.

"Excuse me, Mr Donovan? My esteemed associate and I were wondering if we could buy you a drink," said Evan.

"Actually mate, I'd prefer not to have any company right now. Thanks for the offer though, it's really decent of yah."

I butted in. "Here's the thing Jason; can I call you Jason? My friend here is a huge fan. God knows why, but he is. Anyway, he's a very talented screenwriter. Done a lot of work down in your neck of the woods. You've probably heard of him, Evan Mackleson."

Evan looked visibly uncomfortable and rubbed his eye. Donovan, on the other hand, seemed appreciative of my forthright manner.

"Oh yeah, Evan. Right. Yeah, I've heard good things mate. Pull up a couple of chairs. Please, sit, sit."

"I'll get the beers in," I said.

So far, our improvised Machiavellian designs had worked.

I felt hopeful that my own dream would soon become a reality. The odds were in our favour. Evan had already realised his ambitions and I deduced that my own were likely to come to fruition soon. But it was Steinbeck who'd pondered on the best laid plans of mice and men.

I rejoined the table and found the two men jabbering away like old friends, sharing stories of high school shame and degradation. I'd missed out on the bonding experience and it became plain that I was now the outsider.

"...So Jason, the Sound of Music... How'd ye get roped into that? And in Glasgow at that?" asked Evan.

"Actually mate, I jumped at the chance. It was a pay-cheque for a stage production, which I loved, and I get to see a bit of Scotland, which is great. After I did Joseph and the Amazing Technicolour Dreamcoat, it left me with a taste for musicals."

I placed the beer glasses on the table and we each scuttled our respective drinks in front of us. "Here you go gents!"

"Cheers dude! You're a top bloke."

Evan raised a toast to his boyhood hero and I joined in, sure that I was now part of an exclusive clique. The subject of discussion remained fixed on the highs and lows of Donovan's career, and he spoke briefly about his work in a great Australian soap opera through which he and Kylie had become global stars and household names. In every school playground across the land, kids had pondered the question, 'Will they or won't they?' Just as the focus drew closer on the subject of my desire, he drank down the last of his beer and slammed down the glass.

"Well fellas it's been great chatting, but I've got to get a move on."

He was up like a shot and out the door quicker than a jack rabbit.

"Fucking bastard!" I growled. "He knew we were gonna

ask him about Kylie."

"What a great guy," said Evan.

"Great guy? Did you not see what just happened? He shut us down man! No fairytale pop princess, no glass slippers... not a damned thing!"

"Shut *us* down?" Evan was pissed. "No Max, he shut *you* down! You and your fucked up fantasies. Honestly, you're like a hound in heat!"

I was on the verge of swinging for him, but I restrained myself and managed to hold back. It was a dangerous game to destroy the hopes of a battered soul, no matter how delusional his dreams might be. But Evan didn't know that I was barely hanging on to my sanity by a short and loose thread.

"Let's get back to the rest of the gang," I said, sure that I would be less prone to violent tendencies in the presence of others.

Evan's better half had arrived and was sitting next to Roger, who despite knowing she was unavailable, was doing his best to tempt her toward the dark side. He always swore that women responded to him because of his moustache. It was a sure sign of his masculine virility. But it was obviously failing in this situation. Her every move showed she was uncomfortable with his advances. Evan approached her and stood squarely behind Roger.

"You hittin' on ma bird?"

"Naw. I was just... We were just talking about the Scottish Elections."

"Oh aye? I'd love to hear all about it."

Just as Roger was about to speak the barman hit a large gong and called time on last orders. He'd literally been saved by the bell. We debated for a moment on whether it was worthwhile getting another round in or if it was best to bring the evening to a close. The others all had early mornings, either with work or other errands and it seemed unfair to persuade them to continue on the road to ruin for a night they were sure not to remember.

"Well lads, as always, it was a pleasure and an honour to share a pint or four with you. And even if my plans for this evening didn't quite pan out the way I hoped, it wasn't entirely wasted," I said.

Evans arms were draped over his lady love as she explained where she'd parked the car. She'd stuck to soda and fruit juice, which was wise. The law was particularly strict on such matters and drink drivers were dealt with more harshly than a murderous Manchurian.

I bid my companions a good night and advised them to take care of Jim before leaving the pub. I knew of his predilection for finding trouble. He was at that point, somewhere between being a fun and pleasant eccentric and a mean spirited drunk ready to spit blood. I was in no mood to nursemaid him through misplaced attempts at ego masturbation. I had too many problems of my own.

The full moon shone across the dusty sky. As far as I was concerned, the night was still young and full of possibilities.

13. Deadly Nightshades…
The Scent of Two Roses…

I walked down Sauchiehall Street toward the heart of the city, hoping to find a vibrant hotspot, some hive of social activity. I needed that kind of energy. I fed off it. There, two blocks later, was Club 520. It seemed unusual enough, full of freaks, weirdoes and amateur booze hounds. By outward appearances it wasn't anything special; unless you counted the bright green lights that flooded the pavement in a kind of radioactive glow. A barrage of disco lighting and musical grooves assaulted the eyes and ears of passersby.

I immediately made my way to the bar and commandeered a high chair next to the wood panelled counter. A hefty A4 menu welcomed old and new patrons alike with its colourful list of beverages. I flicked through it for a few seconds and ordered a large Cherry Bomber; one of their many inventive cocktails.

"Go easy on the cherries!" I told the girl.

"I'll bring it right over!" she said.

The whole place was decked out with red patent leather seats and mahogany tables. I sensed the bar staff staring at me from behind the bar and I felt a burning sensation in the base of my neck. The babe who served me tapped me on the shoulder and put down a full pitcher in front of me. The cherries were still bobbing around, gently bouncing up against each other. I asked her for a glass to try the alien concoction.

"Thank you Miss… It certainly looks interesting."

She smiled, held her head in her hands and flicked back her long, lustrous hair.

"My name's Mandy. I work here through the week. Mostly nights. I don't think I've seen you in here before."

"Nice to meet you Mandy. My name's Max. No, first time

in here. I love your hair. It's so... green... But beautiful!" I said.

"Thanks... I think! You seem like a pretty nice guy."

It was obvious she was attracted to the golf trousers. It was only a matter of time before someone, somewhere, developed this kind of sick fetish for them; and here was that someone. Why this relatively intelligent and good looking woman had developed this fascination was beyond me. I'd once read about a man who'd become obsessed with a bicycle tyre in China, with the full intention of consummating the union. There was also the curious case of the French woman who'd married the Eiffel tower. At least this was slightly less unusual. Men often developed strange tastes for articles of female clothing. Was it so wrong that a woman should want to feel the sensation of breathable cotton against her skin?

"You can't have them," I said.

"Can't have what?" she asked.

"Never mind."

She gave me a perplexed look and moved onto serving another customer. I carried on pouring the Cherry Bomber into a tall, thin glass. Fruit juice mixed with vodka goodness. It tasted like a tub of mouthwash. I helped myself to two more servings. After all, I'd paid good money for it. I glanced at my watch. In five hours, dusk would turn to daylight and the bustling city lights would wind down like a carnival shutting up shop. I didn't want to waste what was left of those hours in a club with few redeeming features, except cheap drinks. That would have been a sure sign of an alcoholic.

I finished my tipple and leapt up, ready to explore greener pastures. As I got closer to Hope Street, my head started to swirl and I felt a little woozy. Shadowy images flashed past and I was sure that time itself had somehow slowed down, allowing me to move faster than everything, and everyone, else. But this sensation quickly passed and I soon had a clear idea of exactly where I was going.

Twenty minutes later I was in Mitchell Street. It was a long walk, but my legs didn't feel at all heavy or tired. Diamond Dolls was no ordinary watering hole. The name was the brainchild of some hippy generation porn addict. He'd probably seen too many movies about high-class hookers with hearts of gold and decided to capitalise on the idea. The heat in the night air made standing there unbearable.

Gradually, I made my way through the portal leading into a dimension of depravity. Three well dressed gentlemen, who may as well have had handlebar moustaches, frisked me and I was ushered to the coat check. A hideously obese and unattractive old woman greeted me, took my jacket and gave me what looked like a raffle ticket. The two stout men waved me into the main club hall, but not before issuing a few words of warning.

"No hand contact with the girls."

"Don't worry," I replied. "I won't even touch them with my toes!"

The core chamber of horrors was filled with sweat drenched cannibals pawing at their prey as they garnished them with sticky wads of money. It was an interesting way to get around the rules. It nearly showed a degree of brainpower. The ever changing mood lighting combined well with the suggestive music. It was a far cry from Burt Bacharach's greatest hits, which were my own choice in the realm of seduction. A voice whispered into my ear.

"Hi there stranger. Are you going to buy me a drink?"

I turned round to find a pale brunette barely three inches from me. Her face had a beauty comparable to Julia Roberts and, unlike Shakira, her breasts were easily confused with mountains. She was an 'exotic' entertainer, but there was nothing exotic about her; except maybe her fake fingernails – made in Thailand. She seemed nice enough to share a beverage with.

Her light hazel eyes stared at me. What was she searching for? Miss Super Tits told me her choice of poison; a cosmopolitan with a slice of lime. I was impressed with her selection and ordered the same. She guided me to a vacant booth and I followed her willingly, drinks in hand. I noticed the beer stains on the table and wondered why they didn't have coasters. Maybe they'd been used in a bar brawl. Perhaps some poor soul had been arrested for assault with a deadly beer mat.

"I'm Debbie," she said, crossing her legs and heaving out her cleavage.

"Max," I replied.

I was starting to feel dizzy and dehydrated. Things were moving at a fast pace in the vicinity of vice. I gulped down my Cosmo and laughed nervously, like a deer caught in the headlights of a speeding train. Debbie was completely at ease. She was used to handling all kinds of men in all kinds of ways. Shy or bold, it didn't really matter. We were all just another pay-day.

"Why don't you and me go to the private lounge. We can relax there and I'll perform for you," she purred.

She rubbed her finger down my thigh and pointed to the mythical palace of pleasure. I was unconvinced until Debbie began nibbling on my earlobe. She got up and I followed closely behind, stopping at the bar for our beverages. I held the door open and watched her waddle in. She sat next to me on the black leather sofa that circled the room. This was where improvised entertainment met with skilful dexterity.

"It's fifty pounds for a dance and a hundred for anything else," she said.

I laid some notes down on the table and she signalled to someone through the small window in the door. Mellow music filtered through the wall-mounted speakers as she counted the easy money. She smiled, safe in the knowledge that she'd met her quota for the day. I watched the full hundred disappear into her small black purse.

The show commenced. Debbie used all her honed agility and grace, creating a smooth and sensuous atmosphere. The air seemed heavy again. Her soft, supple body reflected the dim light as she moved with elegance and endearing play. She moved closer and brushed against me. Something caught my eye; a mole maybe. She thrust her breasts into my face. I saw it again, what looked like small punctures on her inner arm. Maybe track marks but I couldn't be sure.

Was she a heroin addict? A thief? A lawbreaking fugitive living in squalor with a pimp called Jaunty? Was he the kind of guy who chewed the bones of golf enthusiasts? My thoughts were scattered and strange visions clouded my brain. It didn't really matter. I gave in to the moment and watched her writhe in ecstasy.

Debbie then straddled me and unbuttoned my trousers. I groaned as she reached in and grappled with my throbbing member. My breathing became faster as her hand moved with a firm intensity, full of purpose. She kissed my cheek and then my bottom lip. Waves of pleasure washed over me and I couldn't hold back.

"Oh God!" I yelled.

Debbie continued, not letting up until I was drained of all my energy. She kissed my forehead and held me against her chest for a few moments. My crotch felt cold and wet as she took her hand away. I wondered if this qualified as breaking the rules. Confusion set in as I watched Debbie riffle through her purse.

"Ah ha!" she said, taking out a handful of tissues.

"Wow, you sure made a real mess!" she giggled, wiping her fingers..

"Yeah. Can I have a couple of those?" I asked.

"Listen, let me at least make sure you get your money's worth. I'll do a couple more dance numbers for you."

"Sure," I said. "You know, with your dancing skills and your head for numbers, you could make it in any field. Except the one where my beloved Cleo sleeps."

"Cleo?" she asked.

"Yeah, Cleo the cow. Get it? Cows & fields?"

She laughed.

"You're not like most of the guys that come here, excuse the pun."

"You're not like most other dancers," I replied.

"Well, I did a few years at Glasgow Uni. Business Management. When the economy started going tits up, I got my tits out. There are only a few jobs that pay as well as this and everyone wants them. Besides, I enjoy dancing here. Mostly."

About an hour later, Debbie's acrobatic display ended in the same fine form it began. My shirt was damp from the salty sweat running down my chest. We'd done every lascivious thing known to man. She winked at me as she put on her frilly black suspenders. I was suddenly overcome with the desire to escape the shame of my mortal soul. Thoughts of Kandy were still swimming in my fractured mind. But the ugly cloud of inner pain went away when Debbie's gentle voice broke through the dark horizon.

"Listen... I don't normally do this... I was thinking maybe... I finish work in half an hour. I don't suppose you'd want to go clubbing afterward?"

I nodded.

"Sure, why not!"

We headed back to the main hall, where a young blonde woman stood waiting with folded arms. She embraced Debbie and the two women talked about hair extensions, eye curlers and something else that was outside my scope of understanding. I stared at the floor tiles for a while.

"Sorry. Katrina, this is Max. Max, Katrina. Kat's from the Czech Republic."

"It's a pleasure to meet you dear lady," I said.

"Hello Maxie! It is pleasure to meet you too,"

She spoke with a slight accent.

"Your English is good," I said, trying not to sound condescending.

"Thank you. I have not been here long. But I read many Harry Potter books and learned much English from them."

Katrina's hair flowed down to her waist. Her slim but alluring figure echoed the shy introvert it embodied. Unlike Debbie, her presence was understated. It catered to those who bought into the illusion of innocence. Her harsh blue eyes showed anything but. They spoke of harsh winters and lonely summers, and a soul sold into bondage for a new country and its currency.

"Katrina, can I get you a small aperitif?" I asked.

"What is that?"

"A drink, dear. He wants to buy you a drink," said Debbie

"Yes, I would like that very much. I will have an orange juice and vodka."

"I'll have the same," said Debbie

I ordered two screwdrivers and an Argentinian beer to keep myself sharp. The women were back to talking about shoes and Cavalli dresses and I was clearly better off out of that whole scene. There wasn't much I could say on that sort of thing and it would have been rude to change the topic of conversation to football. No new punters were coming through the doors. The other dancers spent their shifts persuading unemployed patrons to part with their social security cheques.

I got back to the table and found the ladies giggling like giddy schoolgirls. Had the events that took place in the private room had become a matter of public knowledge? I could feel my throat begin to tighten. Katrina's eyes pierced me with a look that would have made butter melt. An awkward silence followed. She was the kind of woman that a man could easily fall in love with. But I wasn't a man. I was a shell; a bestial cockroach who'd survived the fallout of an emotionally charged nuclear bomb.

When their respective shifts ended, I agreed to meet them outside. They had to freshen up and change into something less respectable and I still had to go back to the coat check to collect my jacket. I fumbled in my trouser pocket for the ticket stub, hoping that I hadn't dropped it somewhere in that labyrinth. The fat redhead with the jowls of a Brazilian boa constrictor scowled at me and handed me my belongings amidst a Jesus based tirade about filth ridden perverts.

I shook my head at the small minded chattering of an ugly old hag who probably hadn't been laid in months; except maybe on special occasions when her pet Labrador consoled her in moments of loneliness. I prepared myself for what was going to be a long night, with more twists than Chubby Checker's dance class.

14. The Devil Disco Dances Where Angels Fear To Tread

Rain fell as I waited outside the flesh pit. The not-so-gruesome twosome certainly took their time. The drizzle added coolness to the suffocating heat and it was a welcome change from the atmosphere indoors. Debbie trotted toward me. I was stunned by her new mode of dress. Her full length skirt flowed down to her ankles. She now looked like a frumpy schoolmarm from an all girls English boarding school. Not longer than twenty minutes before, this perfect vision of womanhood had been busy waxing my wooden carrot.

Katrina broke the silence.

"I feel very hungry."

I was also becoming aware of my own appetite. I hadn't eaten since breakfast. Sustenance had consisted of a liquid diet and stale peanuts. My stomach was beginning to growl. It was no longer possible to survive without solid food. If we didn't find somewhere to eat soon, I was sure I'd be carted away in a box by dawn. And it would be the cheap kind; the kind built from plywood and rusty nails, made earlier by a children's tv show in these macabre times of bizarre entertainment.

There we were, the terrible trio, on an assignment of vital importance; 'Operation-Food-Forage' – classified compartmentalised.

Plenty of take-outs were located around Merchant City, but none were open at that ungodly hour. Fast food had become the cornerstone of our not-so-health conscious society. Most places were second homes to strains of botulism looking for somewhere to hang their hats..

"Let's go to McD's on Jamaica Street," said Debbie. "They'll still be open. You're lucky I'm a cheap date Cassanova!"

"It's a pity that Thai place is closed. You'd have loved it," I said.

"I love Thai!" squealed Katrina.

"I'm more of a breast man," I said glibly.

Katrina laughed. Debbie just shook her head at my impotent humour. Katrina's leopard print shoes shone in the orange street lights. I complimented her on her excellent taste in designer wear. She blushed a little and told me about her obsession with all things Gucci.

We reached McDonalds by around twelve-thirty and ordered four quarter-pounders, one vegetarian meal and a salad. I was out of hard cash and had to use my American Distress card. In times of financial instability, a man's best friend isn't a fluffy puppy, but a cheap piece of plastic with his name, rank and card number printed on it. Imaginary money in a material world.

I picked out a table next to the window. The whole restaurant was deserted. One of the young workers was busy sweeping the floor in preparation for mopping. He was probably an overqualified brain surgeon from Zambia, here in Scotland in search of a better life. Was this it? Cleaning floors, bins and toilets full of human muck. I munched my way through two burgers and stole some of Debbie's fries. Katrina grinned at me, mesmerized by my ability to digest food at an unrivalled rate.

She was still busy with her salad, stabbing tomatoes with a dull fork. The subject of movies came up. My own proclivities for rom-coms were a matter of public knowledge, but this surprised the girls. Their respective tastes for gore and horror were equally shocking. Katrina's personal fascination with vampires unnerved me slightly. I'd often noted that in most horror films, the victims of vampire attacks usually became the predators. This was no exception. Katrina was setting her sights on her newest target: me. I could see she wanted to get her meat hooks into my beef brisket. Debbie's phone chimed twice. She flipped it open and read the text.

"That was my friend Tom. If you're still up for a nightcap, I know this great place where the drinks are cheap and the music's live."

"Sounds interesting," I said, "I'm in."

Debbie and Katrina smirked and stifled their laughter. I'd clearly missed the joke. This was a unique form of torment that I'd often observed in women. My inquisitive nature found it difficult to accept a sense of not knowing. But my masochistic side won out and I didn't press the matter. Clarity would prevail soon enough. I excused myself and went to the bathroom. It was a risk in a joint like this, but my bladder had swelled up like a balloon and I didn't want to trouble the Zambian with another puddle. He looked up at me with sad eyes.

There wasn't enough hand sanitizer in the world to wash away the stench of the shit smelling foulness in the cubicle. The whole experience killed my appetite. The girls had finished their meals and we left. My companions had some trouble keeping up. I was used to walking. Going everywhere by foot had numerous advantages. Not only were we cutting our carbon imprint, but also getting our recommended daily dose of exercise. Unfortunately this was not the foremost thought in the minds of my beautiful friends. Shapely feet came at a price and expensive footwear came at the cost of comfort. But there we were, unwitting eco-warriors, battling the evil of the oil giants and excess oestrogen.

We reached The Polo Lounge, blister free and ready to groove. Our mismatched motley crew sauntered into the building. YMCA was blasting across the floorboards and the designated dance floor was littered with well manicured men in tight jeans and an excellent sense of colour co-ordination. The women sensed I was uncomfortable and cruelly watched on, heckling like hyenas.

Debbie disappeared into the thick of the crowd. Katrina and I stood there, as out of place as two sausages in an ice-cream factory. She tried to say something, but I couldn't hear it over the music. I stared into the crowd and remarked on the liberal use of hair gel. Debbie returned and the two of us breathed a little easier.

"I was talking to the P.A. guy. Tom's going to be on next. You're going to love this Max! He's an absolute darling. Let me get you both a drink. What'll you have?"

"A Southern Comfort on the rocks!"

"Vodka and lime juice!"

"You two wait right here and I'll go get them!" said Debbie

It was wise to be wary of Greeks bearing gifts in these places. There was no telling who or what was lurking in the shadows, waiting to cop a quick feel. Helen of Troy probably felt safer during the Trojan War than I did. But the music gave my limbs a life of their own, and before long, I was jerking and jiving like a chimpanzee suffering sciatic spasms.

I could see Debbie trying to get back to where we were, ducking and diving through an armada of athletic men. With a combination of luck, prayer and skill she made it and hadn't spilled a drop. To our left, I heard two camp crusaders discussing the virtues of Botox.

"We should cull the ugly and extract their DNA for scientific research!" laughed one.

The thought of a harebrained homicidal rampage made me wince. I was not particularly attractive and I knew that I would be first on a hit-list for the aesthetically deficient. The liquor helped calm my nervous disposition.

I began chanting to myself.

"There's no place like home. There's no place like home."

But this only served to get the attention of a hip jiggling youngster who'd barely learned to shave.

"Are you a friend of Dorothy?" he asked, in a seductive tone.

I yelped and clutched my shirt as he twiddled with the buttons.

"I'm not anyone's friend. I'm a vicious bastard!" I replied.

"Hmm. That's just my type!" he said, flashing a lewd smile.

The speaker system suddenly let out a deafening pop. All eyes turned to the MC as spot lights flooded the stage.

"And now ladies, lads and gentlemen, please put your hands together for the Queen of queer, the Dame of delight, from the throne of Vesporia, the Countess Verity Von Glitter!"

There was an unending assortment of wolf whistles and applause. But I was a little confused. I had expected Debbie's friend. Perhaps he would follow afterward. Verity stormed the stage with a horde of bare-chested, well oiled muscular models, all dressed as firemen. A baritone voice reverberated through the bar. I couldn't connect what my ears were hearing and what my eyes were seeing. The image of a dolled-up guy with toilet roll stuffed down his dress proved too much. Katrina moved closer to me and I could feel her heartbeat against my shoulder. I had an erection, but I wasn't sure which of the two things had caused it.

"Hello guys and gals, its time for me to rock this special place and make *your* special place rock hard. Come on my lovely glitter bugs, let's see if you can put out *my* fire!"

I felt like a caveman in shrinking swim shorts. Verity screeched a rendition of 'Raining Men' like a possessed banshee, and the sprinklers went off during the climax. The girls were enjoying themselves.

If there was a supreme deity, he was either ignoring my pleas for help, or on vacation on a remote island. Out of the blue, Verity pointed at me and honed in like a heat seeking missile from a Russian submarine. "Oh, you sad little bunny. Doesn't he look like a terribly sad bunny folks? Why don't you get your cute bum up here and wiggle it for mama!"

My feet were glued to the floor. I couldn't move. Not even to escape this awful nightmare. The crowds parted like the Red Sea and Verity stepped down and grabbed me by the hand before launching me into the glaring spotlight. The women were in hysterics as they watched me get man-handled in the name of entertainment. Finally the demoralising display ended and the drag queen thanked me.

"I hope you didn't mind that bit of bump and grind for these nasty voyeurs."

"It's all in good fun," I said, leaping off the stage and back into the safe womb of anonymity.

Debbie took me aside and explained that Verity was in fact Tom's alter-ego. The physical exertion left me exhausted. Any wasted effort wasn't part of my biological make up. I'd never been one for any sort of manual labour or anything that required a serious use of energy. I needed to sit down.

The night wore on and the live music wound down. Each act was congratulated for an entertaining set. By the final performance most of the customers had left the premises. There were only a handful who were prepared to stay to the bitter end. Verity joined us and Debbie invited her to pull up a chair. I was about to mention something related to fire hazards when I noticed a man gazing menacingly at our group. I'd seen him earlier in the evening and hadn't thought much of it. But there was something disconcerting about his demeanour and body language.

"Ladies, I don't mean to worry you all, but why is that guy staring at us?"

They all looked over at the four foot tall wild man. There was a shock of recognition in Verity's eyes. She sighed.

"That's Edward. He's... he was... a friend," she said as sadness washed over her face.

The shadowy figure moved closer. His forearms were covered in tattoos, the most prominent of which was a large swastika on his left. An alchemical symbol for fire stood out on his right. His psychopathic tendencies were there for all to see – and to fear. I was not at all looking forward to the ugliness that would soon shatter our tranquil mellowness.

"Verity, I... I... I've missed you."

He could speak. For some reason this surprised me.

"Edward, look, this really isn't the time or the place. Maybe we could talk later."

Suddenly a voice said "What's with those fucking tattoos?"

The drink had given me Dutch courage. I knew I was soon going to meet a violent end.

"Who the fuck are you?" he snarled.

"Never mind who I am. Let's talk about who you are. An overt jackass. But no, that would be an insult to all donkey kind. In this case... yes, I think I will take that risk."

I was aware I was speaking the words, but they were independently coming out of my mouth.

"What did you say ye wee prick?"

"You heard me you Nazi bum bandit!"

Vanity interjected.

"Boys, boys please. Look Ed, please don't make this tougher than it has to be."

"Tom... Verity, I don't want to lose you."

"Fine. If you want to do this here and now, then we fucking will! Ed, you weren't the man I thought you were. I can't be with someone so twisted! You're a disgusting homophobe of the worst kind! You couldn't even tell those fucking morons you were gay!"

"I'm not gay! Don't talk about me and my friends like that or I'll..."

His hands started shaking as he balled them up into fists.

"They're patriots who care about our country."

"They're not your friends Ed, they're evil! They don't give a fuck about you, this country or anyone else!"

"Were you dropped on your head as a child?" I enquired.

I knew provoking him was not a smart idea. But I had this odd notion that it was better for me to be in the line of fire than a lady; even if she wasn't actually a lady. I wasn't sure if it was a sense of chivalry, stupidity or a mix of the two.

"Stay out of this you weird fucker!"

"Look, you're obviously a conflicted man. Let me buy you a drink and we'll say no more about it."

He was baffled, but nodded nonetheless. A sense of calm was returned to what had become a toxic and volatile situation. I reached into my pocket and popped two pills from a blister pack, washing them down with the Tennessee whiskey. Verity seemed on edge. Debbie and Katrina hardly said a word except to thank me for their beverages. The tension finally broke

"What were those pills you just took?" asked Ed. "Can I have one?"

15. A Nihilist's Narcotic Nightmare...

I was in a drug and drink filled cocoon, nestled in its warm safety. We were all starting to relax that little bit more. The buzz crept into every crevice of my soul, wrapping itself around me like a warm blanket. I was invincible.

"You fucking foreigners always know where to get the best drugs!" said Ed. "You might be infesting our cities and invading our country, but damn, you know your drugs. I bet you get your hands on the best stuff."

It was true, I did, but I wasn't going to let this sinister bastard have any. He was already high as a kite and out of his Nazi skull. Katrina and I looked at each other, shocked at the ignorance of this half-witted excuse for a human being. Neither of us had spawned from the waters of Scotland; but we were solid citizens, tax payers.

"Ed, I have a question. Why do you hate foreigners so much?" I asked.

"For fuck's sake. Do I really have to spell it out for you? This is the problem with you lot! You come over here, barely able to speak English and steal our jobs. You talk funny, you dress funny... you even *smell* funny. You filthy fuckers have probably never even seen a bathtub! And when you talk to each other in that patois, all you talk about are your plans to take us over! I can't even get a job because of your lot!"

"When did you last actually try and get a job?" I asked.

"Well, there's no point, is there? There's none left for people who are proper British."

"I don't think you believe that. I think maybe you've been *told* to believe that. I mean let's be honest. Even you, being in this bar, that's surely a big no-no in the bible of far right commandments."

He looked awkward and ashamed.

"Well... It is," he said, becoming quiet. An air of thoughtfulness encompassed him. "They talk about it at the meetings, how homos are filthy and sick in the head. I... I don't know what I am, or why I am the way the way I am But It's just not natural. It's wrong. God made Adam and Eve, not Adam and Steve! Christ! I wish I was normal!"

The brain boggling rhetoric that had been pumped into him was spewing out in an uncontrollable torrent of verbal diarrhoea. It had been a long time since I'd witnessed so much hate bottled up in one person. And it was coupled with a self-loathing I'd never witnessed in anyone; except myself. I'd spent a lifetime cornering the market on being a living fuck-up. I was the black sheep in every flock. Perhaps that was why I felt a warped sense of empathy towards him. In his own way, he was as much of a head-case as I was. But he was evil to the bone. It was buried deep inside his marrow.

"Well, you obviously didn't listen to the Beatles much when you were growing up. All you need is love. All love is cool. It doesn't matter where it comes from or where you get it."

Verity's eyes were fixed firmly on the bottom of her glass. She looked at me and smiled.

I pondered the belief systems that led to the waste of what could have been a valuable human being. I knew firsthand how tough it was to let go of any long held dogma. We spend most of our years nursing and nurturing them into adulthood. It doesn't matter that they might be distortions of reality. And then one day, you hear are the silent screams emerging from the agony of quiet desperation; a deafening silence. There, at the edge of that comfort zone, between the dawn of a new day and the darkness of old, are the untamed dogs of war. Then we hope. We pretend that there's some way back to the blackness of ignorance.

Ed was already straddling the chasm, but he wasn't willing to open his eyes to the light. He was a lost cause, doomed to an eternity of pain and prejudice.

The bar-staff were preparing to shut up shop. We gulped down our drinks and prepared to leave. I searched my pockets for a cigarette. We walked as I smoked. None of us knew *where* we were going. There was just this prevailing group mentality. Follow the herd. Wait for the stop sign. Take the first star on the right and straight on until you reach the edge of the cliff. Nevermore land.

Before long, we ended up in the middle of an unfamiliar neighbourhood. I was sure we were somewhere near the Gorbals. Suddenly, we were faced with young thugs demanding our money. The youngest of them, a black teenager with a lisp, waved a hunting knife around.

"Come on, come on, fucking hand it over now! Quickly bitch!"

I reached into my pocket slowly to take out my wallet. Ed looked at him with disgust. The rest of us did our best to comply, hoping to avoid physical harm. The kid threw himself at Ed, blade first. The steely edge of the blade shone in the pale moonlight. The kid was becoming more agitated by the second. He was a reactionary, unlikely to leave it at a simple robbery

I grabbed him by the arm and threw him to the ground, easily wrestling the weapon out of his inexperienced hands and kicked it away. Ed marched toward him, his eyes erupting with volcanic anger. A relentless barrage of punches flew from the enraged psychotic. The boy couldn't defend himself. His comrades abandoned him. The blood from his bruised and beaten face ran onto my shoes. A burst of adrenaline shot through me and I tackled Ed to the ground. The young thug just lay there. He didn't move.

Ed bit at my ankle but I somehow managed to pin him to the pavement. He was considerably larger than an Ecuadorian elephant and twice as strong, but I had no intention of letting him go. His fist delivered a teeth shattering blow.

"You fucking wanker! Get off me!" he yelled.

He was ready to punch me again as I recovered from the shock of the first. After he calmed down, I checked on our injured assailant. He was still breathing. His jersey was stained with whispery black blood, the sheen reflecting the dark deeds of his criminal mind. When he regained consciousness, he ran as fast as his legs could carry him. Disgraced. Humiliated. He'd suffered defeat at the hands of a nihilistic Nazi. Ed was slowly realising that his worst had been witnessed by everyone, including Verity.

"If you'd killed that kid just now, we'd all be sitting in a police cell," I said.

Debbie consoled Katrina, who was distressed by the whole affair. Verity closed her eyes and wrapped her arms around her chest. I put my arms around them and told them that the danger was over. Unfortunately, that was far from the truth. We hadn't just dealt with one psychopath, but two. Ed rambled wildly to himself and let out an anguished roar.

The four of us left him to his fate. I was partly to blame for the whole situation. I'd allowed the malevolent jackass to join us. Now he was a sorry sight; a gay white supremacist, alone, crying a river of tears, mixing with the blood of another human being - Enoch Powell's poster child. His Pit-Bull nature would always be hidden in the vacuous space where a soul should have been.

There was a cab waiting at the taxi ramp. Debbie instructed the driver to take us to her place. None of us seemed in a fit state to be alone.

We clambered up the stairs to her flat. Each of us collapsed on our king-size bed, inebriated and distraught.

Between fits of uncontrollable tears and drunken warbling, I offered the girls samples from my secret stash of pills. Weeping voices; flashes of fuchsia; vivid memories merged with fantasy as images of loveliness bled into my dreams. The seducer was being seduced. I sank happily into the void, unaware of the menace lurking in wait.

I wasn't expecting the descent. Into the bowels of hell itself. Nocturnal horrors. The foul monstrosity that vexed mankind, a great engine of evil, crushing the broken bones of anyone in its way. I could see its limbs sprawled across the globe. It had its claws in every pie, a preternatural entity that knew no bounds. The missing. The dead. Devoured without thought.

Morning.

Katrina was at the foot of the bed wrapped in a sheet. Debbie rolled over and swung her arm around me. I looked at my watch. It was seven o'clock, too early to be up, too late to sleep. I lay there for a while. A familiar voice croaked in my ear.

"Hi."

Debbie was awake. I clung to the duvet as I searched for my Walmart boxer shorts. I found them under the bed. But my shirt and trousers were half way across the room.

"Thank you for last night," she said.

"You're quite welcome."

I squeezed her arm before fumbling with my underwear.

"I should really get going. It's already after eight and I've got so much to do today."

I didn't. But the need to flee was setting in. I'd never been particularly good with morning afters.

By eight fifteen, I was on the bus into town. The fascist bus company that ran the service only took exact change. By the time we reached Glassford Street, my head was empty. I was sure I'd experienced some kind of epiphany, but I couldn't be sure.

Union Street was busy. There was madness on the roads. Rush hour. Angry motorists honked and screamed. Rage driven lunatics, all with somewhere to be, something to do. This sense of urgency turned them into amped up hell-hounds, snarling at pedestrians. I was glad when the twenty three showed up. I didn't want to be in the middle of the incredible ugliness I was seeing. I just wanted to be home.

16. Sammy On Super 8...
Musings On An Overdressed Man...
Bad Memories & Nervous Neurosis...

The phone rang sometime in the afternoon. I gasped, sputtering as I answered.

"Max? Are you alright?"

"Yeah," I said, clearing my throat.

"Oh okay. Good. Have you come down with something? You sound terrible."

"Sammy? Is that you? Man, this is surprise. It's been a while"

"Yes, since the gun totting craziness in Cumbernauld. It was only a squirt gun. I don't know why the police got in such a flap over it."

"Well you have one of those faces. It's painfully obvious to anyone that criminality runs in your veins. It's the face. It gives it away."

"Yeah. I was like 'Jesus, fuck, they're actually going to arrest me for having a toy gun?' I was shitting bricks man!"

"The huge fuck-off camera should have given it away! I mean even a four year-old would know we were filming."

"But you're forgetting one thing. We were in Cumbernauld. They breed the intellectually deficient," I said.

"Yeah. You're not wrong there. And of course there was also that insane homeless guy with the dog.

"The one who'd escaped from a secure psychiatric facility? He didn't make things any easier. He wanted me hung drawn and quartered!"

"It's that MQB energy. You draw these insane types like a dog attracts fleas. Jeff was laughing his ass off over it for three days straight."

"That's true. So anyway, What can I do for you Sammy?"

"Well, I've got this project lined up for the short film festival. I want you in on this."

"Jesus. I'm flattered. But Sammy, there's just one small thing you seem to have overlooked. I'm *not* an actor."

"Nonsense! You're a great actor. Hell, at the very least, you're a character! I want you involved in this thing!"

"Alright, I'll do it. I'll read whatever lines you want me to read. But don't expect me to be happy about it. When do you need me?"

"In a couple of weeks. How's that sit with you? I'll give you the details nearer the date."

"Make sure you have plenty of cheap whiskey. You know I never work without it."

"You got it!"

I'd met Sammy in November of last year. Our mutual friend Jeff had invited me down to Cumbernauld village for a couple of pints in a vain attempt at holding off the winter blues. We drank in a quaint little pub. The locals there had heard of Glasgow, but never dared to venture near it. The thought of travelling to those far reaching ends of the universe and leaving the confines of their homes filled them with dread. It was like a miniature reproduction of the island from 'The Wickerman'.

Thankfully, none of us were left permanently scarred from the incident and lived to tell the tale. Sammy and I forged a bond, despite his being straight laced, sane and very grounded. He had a clarity of vision in his approach to camera work and life. That lager fuelled brainstorming session led to the genesis of Jeff's ambitious and highly unusual idea. The commercial success of films like Shaun of the Dead and the big budget Hollywood film World War Z contributed to the formation of his delusional dream. He said he too would make a zombie movie. His would be the best ever to have graced the silver screen; a Scottish standard bearer by which all future films would be defined. However, he had failed to take into account the true scale of the thing. He also had no script, no cast, no crew, no budget and no camera. But after a long (and occasionally brutal) negotiations with his business partner, Miranda Finkleton, the pair decided that they would embark on this impossible pursuit.

It was January 15th when I got the call. I remember it well. I was sitting at my IBM Selectric typewriter struggling with a story that had been rattling around the back of my brain. It was like a ball-bearing trapped inside a chew toy. I just couldn't get it out and onto paper.

"MQB? It's Jeff. We've put together a team of highly skilled actors for hire. Sammy's doing the camera work. Would you do a small part? Wouldn't involve much work. You in?"

Fuck it, I thought. I wasn't having much luck with writing anything. In the last three months, the only thing I'd produced was a three line poem, which was published twice and read on radio. But I knew just like most, it was in actuality, complete and utter horse-shit.

"Sure," I said, "I'm in. You know my rates. Booze and broads."

"You'll get both. I'll make sure of it. Even if I have to hire the hookers myself. Now get your ass down here on Tuesday at 7pm."

The remainder of that January was filled with train trips to and from the village of the damned. I fondled beautiful women outside of working hours and drank myself into a stupor with the free flowing supply of Tennessee whiskey. In rare moments, between madness and brief flashes of clarity, I would read lines from a large printed sheet, stapled to a board or camera stand, mumbling incoherently while I watched Jeff swell up like a toad.

"That's fabulous! Just marvellous darling! I've never seen such deliciousness ooze out of a man and into the camera!"

Jeff was supposedly straight and married, but he had the curious habit of wearing his wife's cardigan. This puzzled us all greatly. Undertones of cross-dressing freakishness pervaded through the entire production process. Most of the cast tried to dismiss this weird behaviour, putting it down to issues of weather and staying warm. But we all knew there were countless jumpers and jerseys designed for gentlemen that met these requirements. When Jeff grew a long John Holmes style moustache, a flurry of questions arose surrounding his sexuality and frame of mind. Suspicions were banded about and Chinese whispers had blown the rumours into the realm of the ridiculous: a guy who knew a guy saw him groping a bearded man in a cotton shirt.

The sensible ones among us tried to ignore this terrible gossip. We were told we had to be serious actors because we had serious parts; and we had standards to maintain. At the end of the gruelling film shoot, it ended up in post-production hell and no-one, not even Jeff, knew exactly when his project was going to hit a projector screen. This didn't bother me particularly. I'd already gotten my rocks off and snagged seven free cases of whiskey and five crates of beer, which lasted until the end of the month.

Those hard nights of rigorous rehearsals and never ending retakes were a strange but special time. Friendships blossomed, ideas mushroomed and inspiration struck. There was lunacy in every undertaking. But we followed our true spirit paths. We were making art. Six months later, the soul of it was still alive and kicking. Our drive and determination had been distilled, bottled and pumped back into us intravenously. One hundred percent pure concentrated coolness in our veins.

I was looking forward to working with Sammy again. But I had no clue what his new project was. It may have involved shooting high definition candid shots of monkeys masturbating in space. Whatever its nature, it was sure to be interesting, with just a hint of overall lunacy. It's that same insanity that pushes a kid from Govan to steal stereos and television sets from the homes of the better off. A renegade spirit, refusing to be caged or cajoled with promises of gainful employment and a subservient suburban lifestyle. It revels in the joy of freedom; the freedom to do what it likes, when it likes.

But this romanticised notion also makes it as dangerous as it is attractive; especially in the realms of crime. Sometimes creativity and crime fused, resulting in violent sociopathic tendencies; the desire to commit the perfect murder artfully, a masterpiece of illegal action. I walked that fine line of unpredictability; between genius and being mentally deranged; between good and evil.

A Non-Educated Delinquent; a NED. That's what they'd branded me all those years ago. And it remained invisibly tattooed on my forehead like an emblazoned emblem; my badge of honour. I was a troublemaker, a hoodlum, a reckless escapee from a lost generation. I watched my mother cry as they read out the long litany of my indiscretions and alleged activities. Courts, schools and prison had done nothing to change the nature of my character. No-one had bothered to ask *why*. They talked a lot. Social workers, teachers, doctors with plenty of fancy certificates and diplomas.

I was misunderstood, they said. They wanted to 'understand' me, like some newly discovered species in the Amazon. Men in white coats tried to dissect me with blunt tools in a sealed off lab.

At sixteen, with no home and a family that wouldn't accept me back into its folds, I enrolled in the British Army. A few months of basic training later, I found myself in the middle of

Bosnia. It was my first foray into the world of adulthood; a war-zone. I was completely unprepared for it. Senseless killing, rape and torture were the norm. There are no words to convey the true horror of the thing, because the only people that understand it are the ones who have been there.

By nineteen, I was honourably discharged on medical grounds. Post-traumatic Stress Disorder. Just another problem in an ever growing list that had to be overcome. I was already self-medicating with heavy boozing sessions and a series of bear-knuckle brawls in bars across town. I had no job, no money and no qualifications. All I had in my wallet at that point was my driving license, five pounds and a rail ticket from Glasgow to London. I met Susan not long after boarding the train. She was a svelte redhead with big blue eyes and a petite posterior that caught my attention almost immediately. I bought her a drink and a bag of peanuts before telling her that I'd just spent the last of any money I had. We chatted for a while before adjourning to the bathroom for a quick fuck. When we reached London, she offered me a place to stay and I accepted graciously.

I moved into her one bedroom hovel, where space was limited, electricity was a privilege and screaming matches were held regularly. The convenience of sex and the need for companionship suited us both. I took up work as a waiter and got other odd jobs wherever I could, as long as they didn't require any reading or writing. I couldn't do either. I remembered how in school the four-eyed experts had diagnosed me with autism. They said it was the root cause of all my behaviour. Utter bullshit. But they may have been right about the cognitive effects.

Susan suffered from schizophrenia, which in itself was not a major issue. But she hadn't followed her doctor's advice and went five weeks without taking her medication. Our arguments got worse and things reached boiling point when she picked up a frying pan and brought it down on my head.

A short hospital stay later Susan and I called it quits and I left for Manchester, where life didn't get any easier. Some gangster wannabes roped me into helping them in their efforts to take over the turf of a rival racketeer. I was fine with that. By that point I'd generally lost the will to live, thinking that it was better to go out in a blaze of glory. A part of me still feels this way, and a dramatic suicide is never entirely off the cards.

Stuff got heavy when they brought shotguns into the equation. These things were fairly commonplace, but I'd lost my taste for unnecessary bloodshed and decided to leave before I found myself with another gun in my hands, destined to fire its bullets into the back of someone's skull.

Those early years did have some up sides. I was fortunate enough to run into an old friend who'd established himself as a legitimate computer repair specialist. He'd expanded his modest empire into a three outlet thriving business. He offered me steady employment as a cleaner. I was desperate enough to do almost anything. His kindness extended beyond that. He knew of my fondness for the New World. I had some extended family there, hailing from my mother's side. He filed the paperwork for emigration and ticked all the necessary boxes. I didn't think it would come to anything, but within a year, I was bound for the great state of New York.

For the next two years, I made Trenton, New Jersey my home. It was noisy, filthy and frequently subject to drive-by shootings. On a couple of occasions the sound of a car backfiring scared me so badly that I took cover behind a garbage can. Sadly, my distant family didn't want to know me; not because of my acquired reputation; but because of the fact that my mother had married my father. They'd disowned her for that. It was ironic.

I was holding down three jobs, but I made sure I took one

day off every week. It was on one of these days in late July that I discovered the New York public library system. As a boy, I'd never set foot in one. They used the Dewey decimal system, which boggled the hell out of me. I'd watched a lot of Hammer horror movies and especially liked Christopher Lee's overly dramatic acting in Dracula. I knew the story was based on the book by Bram Stoker and wanted to read it. I remember feeling embarrassed by my own ignorance when asking the librarian for help in finding it. The old lady was good enough to show me where it was and I quickly learned how to find other books in that text-rich maze. I also checked out a dictionary and spent the next eight months learning to read.

I soaked up words like a sponge, expanding my vocabulary until I was sure I'd used every word in that dictionary; particularly the rude and offensive ones. They came in handy on those unkind streets. At night, after finishing work as a toilet attendant, I would spend two hours writing out the words one-by-one. It's fair to say that my handwriting was, and to this day remains, atrocious. Books on grammar and punctuation followed, but those were considerably more difficult to understand. There were numerous rules on what went where, how and why. It was slow progress.

17. A Scottish History X...

In October of 1925, a child was born in a small village in the Punjab on the Indian subcontinent. He was the son of a poor and humble bricklayer during the age of the British Raj. Everyday for eight hours, three hundred and sixty-five days through the year, he toiled in the hot baking sun. He carried concrete blocks and building bricks on his back to cement his future foundations. The going rate for his sought after service was the equivalent of fifty pence an hour in today's money, which was more than what most were earning. The job market was oversaturated with uneducated and unskilled workers, and any prospect of employment depended heavily on the concepts of natural selection; only the fittest survived.

Such was the strength and spirit of this father that he frequently sacrificed his daily bread so his wife and son could eat. He had almost nothing in the way of worldly possessions, little in the way of creature comforts and lived a simple life in a small mud hut. There was however, one item that he always kept by his bedside, a small pamphlet depicting individual letters of the Hindi alphabet, given to him by a childhood friend as a gift when he was about fourteen. With those tattered bits of paper, he taught himself how to read and passed that knowledge on to his son, whose thirst for learning exceeded his own.

This full-time labourer was also the village weightlifting champion. The Schwarzeneggers of modern times have precision made barbells and dumb-bells, conforming to safety checks and health regulations. But back then, in those backward times, they didn't have those sorts of things. Instead they used the heaviest boulders they could find from nearby farmlands, and lifted them above their heads before tossing them as far as possible. By all accounts, a man could easily be crushed underneath one. But the years he'd spent hauling inhuman loads gave him a hide tougher than leather and a will stronger than steel. He was the original Iron Man and he didn't need a suit or a Mr Universe prize to prove it. But eventually ill-health and old age caught up with him and he was left bedridden.

His son was no less a man. By the age of eighteen, he'd educated himself to be fully fluent in his mother tongue and had also learned to write in several other languages, including Hindi, Urdu and Sanskrit. He was the first in the village capable of speaking a few words of broken English; which got him noticed. The people elected him as a kind of spokesperson in a tribal system of politics. By then he was single-handedly carrying the burden of the bricks that his father had carried before him. When the old man finally passed away, he took on the full responsibilities of the former, but continued in his study of the English language by enrolling in formal classes at a school in a nearby town.

There's a story that's often told about this man by his friends: one day when he was in that town he saw a scrawny holy man scavenging for scraps. With his begging bowl in hand, he sought alms from a British soldier, proudly wearing his smart, starched uniform. The soldier kicked the beggar away and mercilessly beat him like a mistreated dog. The little man had all seven shades beaten out of him. The beggar seemed more concerned with picking up the pieces of his broken bowl. It sounds funny that a man should do this, but on thinking about it, it was probably the only thing he owned. Our native moralist, now armed with the basics of the English language, walked up to the soldier, snatched the baton from his hands and said softly, "You knocked him down. Why don't you try knocking me down." Shamed and scared the soldier ran away, presumably into the arms of his mother to cry about how the big bad indigenous man had scared the poor Imperialist swine. That man was my grandfather.

Some years later, news of war came to the village and men were being asked to volunteer for the British Army to fight a most dangerous threat in a far away land. My grandfather was the only educated man residing there and had read newspaper articles on the Nazis and the heinous wrongs they were visiting upon countless souls. Most were indifferent to what was going on. It was Europe, thousands of miles from their doorstep and they were still busy fighting for their own freedom from British rule. Some were still mourning the atrocity of the massacres at Amritsar, where innocent blood had been shed by a well armed, cruel militia. But my grandfather had met Gandhi and seen him take up the fight against oppression and tyranny in his own homeland. To him, two wrongs didn't make any kind of right. So when the call of duty came, my grandfather answered. His sense of justice and ethics super-seeded his pride. His own conscience wouldn't let him sleep at night unless he did something to oppose the scourge of the Third Reich.

His fiancé didn't understand and rowed with him in what he often called 'her great fit of foolishness'. They'd met during the summer months when he'd worked for her father. My grandfather was not a romantic, though some say he was known for his legendary prowess as a lover. The two were set to be married by the end of that year. I think deep down he knew that she didn't want to see him become another casualty of a bloody war that showed no signs of ending. Nonetheless, he didn't allow his personal feelings to sway him. He put down his bricks and picked up a rifle.

In 1952, after doing his duty and travelling the world, he came back to his beloved India, which by then had been divided into three states, with boundaries of religion, class and creed separating whole families. Mob mentality had taken over at the height of the troubles and the murder of women and children was commonplace. He tried to understand the reasons behind the mass killings. Why had things had gone so hideously wrong between people who had once stood together, even fought together for their motherland, their Bharat? What should have been a simple transfer of sovereign power had descended into angry anarchy. He poured over past newspapers to find answers but found nothing that could answer these burning questions. My grandmother later told me that it was the only time she'd ever seen this powerful man cry.

Some years and two kids later my father was born. He had no patience for education and no stamina for hard work. He spent most of his time playing with chickens and chasing girls. He had some schooling but preferred his own company to sitting with other kids in stuffy classrooms. My grandfather took up work as a desk clerk in the same nearby town where he'd received his formal education and was given living quarters the size of a shoebox by his employer. There was no way his family could stay there. His wife and children elected to stay in the village. Being the primary wage earner, he spent little time in the family home. The wages were pitiful, but he tried to save as much money as he could, though occasionally he did take trips back to the village.

By 1975 my father had met my mother, a Jewish woman whose family had settled in the neighbouring town before the war. They were completely against the relationship and vowed on everything holy that they wouldn't accept my father because of his Muslim heritage. But this didn't dissuade my parents. At the time they married, India was at war with Pakistan, the cold war had begun and crops were failing throughout the region. My grandfather had spent his savings on an elaborate wedding ceremony. Things looked grim. Food prices began to soar, living costs shot up, and work was scarce. When the small firm he worked for went bankrupt, my grandfather took the grave decision to move his family out of the village and into a proper city, the nearest of which was some hundred miles away. He was sure that work could easily be found there and he was right.

Like many others searching for the pot of gold at the end of the rainbow, they ended up living in a small slum, under tin huts with leaky roofs. My grandfather quickly found work, but again it didn't pay particularly well. My father was unsuccessful in finding any gainful employment due to his lack of qualifications. When my mother had me, they were barely eating a meal every three days. It was around then that a close friend of my grandfather's, who'd served with him in the war, had the good fortune of meeting him at a political rally and told him of how he could take reach the magical land of England. My grandfather borrowed money from a disreputable loan shark and lodged an application with the British Embassy. The Empire had robbed his country of its resources and asked him to fight a war on its doorstop. Why, he asked himself, shouldn't he take advantage of this opportunity to get something back; a chance at a decent life for himself and his family?

We arrived in Birmingham some years later, but found it difficult to acclimatise ourselves to another country with completely different cultural norms and terrible weather to boot. Value systems clashed, language barriers stood in the way and racism was rife. But it was still the land of opportunity, where work was plentiful and wages were such that a man could live like a king; or at least his servant. It wasn't long before our nomadic ways took us from Birmingham to Milton Keynes, and finally northwards to Scotland.

By the time I was seven we had settled in the city of Glasgow. I knew little in the way of English and at school I was considered to be one of the 'special' children. My younger brother, who'd been born some years previous, had by then been diagnosed with a rare disorder known as Thalassemia. It was similar in nature to sickle-cell anaemia. The body can't produce the required red blood cells that carry oxygen to the vital organs. It's not a serious problem when a person is afflicted with the minor variant. But when two afflicted people have children, the chances of a child developing the major condition are greatly increased. However, things like this were not widely understood in those days and especially not by the generally uneducated populace from third world countries.

Countless blood-transfusions followed and appointment after appointment with specialists, GP's, and nurses yielded no long-term solutions to the problem. Finally, a bone-marrow transplant was deemed to be the only option. They took blood samples from each of us and checked them for matches. I was too young to understand most of what was going on, but I got the general gist of it. That was when they laid it on me. I was the only match due to my not having either the minor variant or any other medical issues. They asked me if I understood what that meant, the implications of the whole procedure. I didn't, but I said I did. The only thing that I knew was that I had the chance to save my brother's life. And so I agreed to be the bone-marrow donor. During the early '80's, the transplant methods were nowhere near perfected. The risks were extraordinarily high and Thatcher's government cutbacks meant that funding for the National Health Service was not what it should have been.

My mother and father argued night and day on the pros and cons of the decision and neither seemed completely happy, nor willing to go through with it. Yet, there seemed to be no alternative. The doctors took great pains to explain how, without the operation, my brother would slowly lose all his faculties as he grew older. I would find out in the years to come that this was not entirely true. Many people with the condition lived relatively normal lives with their faculties fully intact, as long as they underwent regular transfusions and were monitored carefully. The procedure itself was later perfected and in modern times, the risk factor was reduced to a minimum.

Sadly, not being hopeful of what the future might bring (most of the country was experiencing a blanket pessimism in those days) my parents chose to take the doctors' advice and we were both admitted into hospital for the operation and anaesthetised before surgery. I remember groggily waking up in the middle of the operating theatre and someone saying "He's awake! Can you increase the dosage?" and I lost consciousness again. When I woke the second time I was in an uncomfortable bed inside a curtained cubicle. I got up, walked around and asked the orderlies where I could find my family. My brother was in a sealed room with 'Intensive Care Unit' labelled on the door. Something had gone wrong. There was panic etched on everyone's face. My father sat solemnly outside the room, holding his head in his hands. My mother didn't say anything but wept a great deal.

A man in a surgical mask came out of the room, crouched down next to me and said, "He wants to see you."

He patted my shoulder as he guided me into the cleaning area and made me wash my hands. The room was white with a plastic feel and the floor stank of bleach. The frail boy opened his eyes and spoke a little, asking for water. The guy in the mask went to fetch it. My brother picked up his metal cereal bowl and threw it at my head with the might of a Japanese sumo wrestler. I could have choked the little bastard then and there, but instead we both burst out laughing, throwing whatever came to hand at each other. We shared the same sick sense of humour, but I can honestly say that he outdid me in every act of misbehaviour. The nurses were not at all pleased at having this feral child on their hands, but he made them smile and they in turn developed a strong affection for him.

In the spring of 1989, as the Earth was coming to life, his body withered away. He died peacefully in my mother's arms in the middle of March. The funeral service was short and some of the hospital staff even put in an appearance; at least the ones who could make it. The ones who couldn't also sent cards and letters of condolence. My grandfather in particular was grief stricken by the death of a grandchild. He used to call us his 'champions', and I'm sure his friends got tired of hearing about the awesome daily feats of his personal gladiators. He'd tell everyone how we'd stomped on some classroom bully or bitten some gloved dentist who insisted on using archaic torture devices on innocent children. He never seemed to mind our wayward ways, even when our parents scolded us for being 'uncontrollable'.

I personally cried continuously for four days before a sense of melancholy washed over me. A big part of me died along with my brother. The sky seemed a little darker without one of its brightest lights shining on this mortal coil. I never shed another tear after those days of mourning.

My father's temper became more frightening as he struggled to deal with the loss and my mother just stopped speaking, lying in a catatonic state through the passing hours. I didn't mind the beatings and in a way, I looked forward to them as a break from the emptiness that filled the house. I often wished and sometimes daydreamed of what it would be like to live in the school I went to at the time instead of that god-awful home. I even convinced myself that I must have been adopted; that my real family was out there somewhere, people that actually loved me. My grandfather spent a month explaining to me that this was not the case.

There was one particular day. Nothing exceptional about it. I was walking through the park at the end of a long school day. I was stopped by a group of young thugs yelling things like "Paki scum", "Darkie" and "Black bastard". I tried to go around them but before I knew what was happening, I was being punched in the face repeatedly. They spat on me then left me on the wet grass to nurse my wounds. I got home sometime in the late evening and I remember my first thought was to check on my mother. My father was out, I wasn't sure where or why, but I was grateful for the reprieve. I probably wouldn't have been able to take too much more blunt force trauma that day anyway. My mother glanced over at me with her sunken eyes, bundled in a quilt, covered in the eerie stench of the grim reaper. She hadn't touched her breakfast, which was still lying in the same plate it was in that morning on the small wooden tray next to her bedside. I went to the bathroom and cleaned up with soapy water.

As usual my homework was still lying undone in my backpack. I had no plans on actually doing it. It consisted of composing sentences for words the teacher had scrawled in white chalk across the blackboard. There was no way I could complete the task, but I had something else on my mind as I was scrubbing the mud and spit off my face. There was one word that the kindly old woman had taken great pains to explain as she wrote it for the class. "Hate" in big bold letters as the chalk squealed on the dry board. It may seem strange, but I'd never before thought of myself as being any different from anyone else before then. But I realised that I was. Seen as less than people with a lighter skin colour. It's really not the kind of epiphany you would want to have at a young age.

I can't say how I managed to get through those testing times, because my memory of the years after is splintered. What I do know is that my parents divorced not long after my tenth birthday. My own reaction to these things was not good and I ended up involved with all kinds of nefarious activities.

I didn't see my father again for many years and my mother's general state of health, both mental and physical, declined over a period of time. The worse she got, the more I reacted. I kept hoping that something would get her attention and that she'd wake from the stupor that kept her in a cloud of depression. Eventually, this tactic worked and after being arrested, charged and taken to juvenile court, she finally got upset enough to throw me out of the house and into the gutter. We never spoke again. My grandfather, being the only constant in my life, was a voice of wise counsel and reasoned gentleness, and he persuaded me to try doing something useful with my life.

Whilst walking past a poster and a recruitment officer, I decided to sign up and "Be the best!" The polished foot-soldier in his full-dress uniform insisted that "It's not just a job, it's an adventure!" The fact that I had no formal education, however, posed a problem. But this was easily overcome with a battery of aptitude tests and a medical check-up. I was a little stunned when they told me I had a high Intelligence Quotient despite my obvious impediments. Perhaps they'd confused my results with those of some other recruit? But it got me three square meals, a bed and a steady income and I wasn't about to complain.

The years went by fast. At the age of eighty-two my grandfather passed away unexpectedly in his sleep. He was surrounded by loved ones and the greatest of friends. Everyone was there; except for me. I was in New York when it happened, but I flew in for the funeral. I met my father again and we spoke briefly. He was older and greyer than I remembered, but he'd aged well otherwise. He seemed more settled and stable than the man I'd known as my dad. He told me that my grandfather had left me a recording which he wanted me to hear after his death, along with some other various nick-knacks, including his war medals and a journal.

I took the cassette with me back to New York and it remained sitting there on a small writing bureau for some months before I eventually found the courage to play the thing. I listened intently as my grandfather's voice spoke to me from beyond the grave. He told some amusing anecdotes and a fart joke. He always liked to keep things light. As the machine played on, his tone became more serious as he described in detail his life and times. I began to notice the parallels between his life and my own and gained a sense of comfort from just hearing the sound of voice. At the end of the tape he told me he was proud of the man I had become.

"Above all else," he said, "a man must live like a lion and love like he means it."

That tough Punjabi lion had gone up to the spirit in the sky and left this world in a better state than he'd found it in. There was something funny in the fact that he'd made Glasgow his adopted home; the city was an asphalt jungle with just as many dangers as the undiscovered regions of the Amazon. But its coldness had taught me how live, how to survive and how to eat. The salt on its streets, my streets, was mixed in with my blood. Our story, my story, was but one amongst a million; from Generation X to a Scottish history X, consigned to antiquated history books with broken spines.

18. Sherwood In The Forest Reads Rabby The Hood...

'They've taen a weapon, long and sharp,
And cut him by the knee;
Then ty'd him fast upon a cart,
Like a rogue for forgerie' – Robert Burns, John Barleycorn: A
Ballad

I slithered into my bedroom, in a funk from unearthed memories that were best left buried. I couldn't sleep, tossing and turning, desperately trying to get to that mellow zone so I could slip into the slimy pool of my subconscious. The pillows were Egyptian cotton and the sheets were silk lined. But it made no difference. I stared at the ceiling, watching bits of peeling plaster curl into weird shapes that came alive for brief moments. The sound of passing traffic built into a crescendo of incoherent wailing. I grew accustomed to it. It's reassuring in those dreadful moments when you're all alone with only your thoughts for company. They begin talking to you.

"Look at you. Why are you breathing. Let it go. You know you want to."

The dissonance drowned out the demons. High-hat drum beats burst through the thin film of slumber, crawling up my spine and biting hard into the nerve endings, Lady Gaga screeching like a poltergeist. It confirmed my suspicion that the woman upstairs had bad taste. Did she have to assault my senses with the atrocious auto-tuned ravings of a half-baked hell-hound?

There's nothing more infuriating than being in the throes of a brain bending migraine and having an inconsiderate neighbour torture you in a way that probably goes against the Geneva Convention. Soon I'd start gnawing on balls of twine and talking to giant imaginary cockroaches; all in the vain hope that stamping on them will offer some relief.

The state of heartbreak, coupled with temporary insanity, makes a man do curious things. For instance, the act of kidnapping and molesting your neighbour's pet hamster with a cooking utensil is not one that occurs to your ordinary person. But in desperate circumstances, one resorts to sick and desperate measures.

Once the deed was done, I slipped into my piss-stained slip-on shoes, ready to give the bitch a piece of my mind. I'd put up with her bullshit long enough. Week in, week out for months on end, it was always the same thing. Music blaring at three o'clock on a Monday morning. Then there were those joyous afternoons when my walls would shake like a Las Vegas whorehouse..

I grabbed the golf club I'd placed next to the door for protection purposes and went up. I rang the doorbell with violent abandon and rapped the knocker mercilessly. Spit bubbles were forming at the corners of my mouth. I was a savage animal. I heard something smash and then someone wrestling with the deadbolt. The door flew open and there she was, dressed in a yellow Lycra jumpsuit. She looked sexy as hell.

"Do you know how loud your bastard music is?" I yelled.

"What!?"

She seemed alarmed at the sight of the golf club in my hand.

A red mist descended and I stormed into her home, quickly locating the CD player. A succession of well honed blows led to its destruction and it ceased squawking immediately. This was the result of perfecting my handicap on the golf course.

"You're going to pay for that! I'm going to call the police!" she screeched.

I spun round to face her.

"No, you won't," I said, grabbing her waist.

I tipped her over and kissed her firmly on her pale lips. She didn't fight it. I was inclined to fuck her there and then.

"Send me the repair bill and get another one, but for fuck's sake, keep the volume down. There's a button on it for a reason; use it!"

She smiled as I left.

I was too wired to sleep so I caught up on my emails instead. The computer was a basic junker I got from 'Junkie Jack'. I didn't use it very often but it was a handy way of keeping in touch with people, and it added to my otherwise bare living space.

I scrolled through the offers for Viagra and penis extensions that flooded my inbox regularly. Most of these were hustles of one sort or another. I knew of one friend who'd been gullible enough to 'buy' a Russian mail order bride. Next thing he knew, his credit card had been charged for three large screen televisions, a thousand dollars in traveller's cheques and subscriptions to Asian porn channels in Vietnam. Those sneaky fraudsters always had some kind of hook for what their 'phishing' scams.

When most of the rubbish was deleted, I saw an email from Matt Sherwood. Matt was a well respected member of the Writer's Foundation. How the devil did he get my email address?

"Hi Max. Find your stuff very interesting. Could use tweaking. Don't know if you've heard, Forest Cafe in Edinburgh is set for closure. This would be a great loss to the Scotland's grass roots counter-culture. Many fine artists, writers and poets have found a home there and gone on to greener pastures. Hosting a fund raising event to get a 'Save the Forest' collection going. Can we rely on to support it? Would be great if you could be there as a guest speaker. Tomorrow 6.30pm. Thanks, Matt."

I checked the date on the email. It was sent yesterday. It was already a half past three. If I got cleaned up and left soon, I might just make it. The train would take at least an hour to get there, and getting from here to Queen Street would take around thirty minutes. I was going to need a lot of caffeine to stay alert and awake among that crowd. They were perfectly decent people, but they were all so stale and dull that doctors ought to have marketed their events as the perfect cure for premature ejaculation. On and on they would droll, searching for acceptance, applause and adoration from the same five people that showed up over and over again. It was a grotesque example of the 'X-Pop-factor-Idol-Big-Brother' culture that had been cultivated by privileged Baby Boomers. 'Get rich quick!', 'Claim your fifteen minutes of fame!', 'Be in the spotlight'.

I had no time for that sort of thing. Under other circumstances, I wouldn't have bothered. But Matt was one of a rare breed; an exceptionally talented lovey of the upper class crumpet munchers. This made him a bit of a pompous prick, but I had a profound respect for his writing style; balls out and brash. In many ways he was similar to Truman Capote. It surprised me that he hadn't reached the same heights as the former. But then, one never quite knows what tomorrow will bring. The future is long.

My coffee had percolated nicely. I mixed in the sugar and cream and clouds of white infused in the mug. Wisps of dairy goodness streaked up to the top like marble tiled patterns of the Venus de Milo. I stirred it slowly as I watched the sun break through the murky grey sky. The rain had stopped sometime earlier and it looked like summer was finally coming back in force.

The sweet sounds of Anthony Hamilton's motown music

grooved through the radio and into the ether. There was a peculiar scent in the air. I sniffed out the source of the terrible odour: it was me. I smelled like an Albanian goat herder who'd spent the morning molesting chickens.

At four o'clock, I emerged clean and dressed in a pair of boot-cut jeans and a beige turtleneck that clung to me like cling-film. By the time I got to Queen Street, my left leg had a cramp.

The large board overhead flashed with various departure times and platform numbers. The train leaving for Edinburgh was due to leave at 4.55pm. That gave me a good twenty minutes at least. It took almost all of that time before I got to the front of the queue. I stuffed the two ten pound notes into the automated ticket machine. Clank. Buzz. Screech.

I went through the turnstiles and waited patiently on the platform. The train was cramped, but I was lucky enough to find a seat before the deluge of last minute commuters piled on. I was beginning to regret wearing cotton. The combined body heat of all the passengers made the temperature soar. Soon the whole carriage was like a parched desert and I was tempted to strip down to my shorts whilst applying liberal amounts of lotion to my bulging gut.

I rested my head against the back of the seat. The driver announced the various stations. Falkirk and Haymarket were mentioned, but the rest became a blur. Nothing but endless rows of fields and the occasional hill. The placid and peaceful countryside. The most interesting sight was a man probing a sheep's orifice. I assumed he was a veterinarian. The alternative explanation seemed too disturbing to think about.

We arrived in Edinburgh, Waverley at six o'clock on the dot. Out onto North Bridge and then towards Cowgate. I'd always thought it strange that they'd given a street such a weird name. I passed by the Cabaret Voltaire. I had fond memories of that place.

Between it and the Banshee Labyrinth, Scotland's capital had a stronghold on excellent boozers.

The University grounds near Chambers Street were astounding. That curious combination where history met modernity. Old bell towers next to glass windowed shopping complexes, beautifully crafted stonework next to cruel and unusual apartment blocks. The same thing was happening everywhere. Tourists in Edinburgh still got the authentic feel of its past, but in Glasgow most of the old buildings and hallowed churches had been desecrated by monstrosities that stood in their place.

And then there was Edinburgh's re-introduction of the old tram system, responsible for the chaotic destruction of many roads. The cost had spiralled out of control; beyond the £4 million mark. Allegations of back-handers in local council circles were ever emerging. But there was nothing wrong with the initial idea. It had a certain quaint appeal to history buffs like me. As some in the Scottish Parliament had pointed out, it was an efficient form of public transport. But were we really prepared for the birthing pains required for this transformation?

I turned right then took the second left, zigzagging past the hordes of work-tired passers-by. You could tell they'd put their noses to the grindstone; a hard day's graft. Even the bums wore looks of exacted strain as they begged for copper coins. I knew something about hard knocks. But that was another life. Rough-sleepers in this new age had it worse. The mathematics of economics: rising inflation equals less two pence pieces in their Styrofoam cups. They'd soon have to sing for their supper; 'dance monkey, dance'.

The rest of the world didn't give a fuck. They were too busy trying to stave off starvation in their own countries, which were all one step away from a complete meltdown. I pressed a ten pound note into the hand of a dishevelled woman. She muttered something about it being too much and thanked me profusely with drugged up blessings, like a Sufi on a Persian carpet in the mystic east. She was just another invisible member of society. Not even a face in the crowd, unheard and unwanted. A non-recognisable name blanked out of vision by those with Passports, birth certificates and National Insurance numbers. Did she even exist? Was she really here? Just 'dust in the wind'.

I reached a fork in the road near the Bedlam Theatre, across from the Forest Cafe. People had congregated in the anteroom inside. They all pretended to know each other well; shaking hands with strangers they'd seen once at some stage play; brushed off politely by those with status. Besides Matt, no-one knew who I was, which suited me just fine. I hadn't planned at all for this eleventh hour affair. My first thought was to make up some gibberish on the spot when my name was called, say whatever came to mind, then leave as quickly as possible without being held up by these zealots of the written word.

It all hinged on one thing; not having my name called until the end, when hopefully these bastards would be too tanked on Strongbow and red wine to notice my eccentric ravings. But my strategy was scampered when Matt decided to announce me as the first speaker of the evening. There I was, just through the door and I had to deal with this dire situation. Two volunteers with collection tins stood next to the stage. Middle-class morons threw in bundles of cash they couldn't afford to burn, just so they didn't look out of place. They wanted to be hip, one of the in-crowd. It was sickening. I scrambled up the steps, took hold of the microphone and rocketed into a rant of epic proportions, saying anything that came to mind.

"I'm not sure what I'm supposed to say here... I'm suffering from a drink and drug induced headache... accompanied by hallucinations of aliens with an unhealthy obsession of probing Earth cattle. Let me tell you, extra-terrestrials are real sickos!"

There was nothing. Not even the white of a tooth. I continued. "Well, this morning I destroyed my neighbour's sound system and thought out a series of pick-up lines for donkeys in heat. Don't worry about my neighbours; they're all evil Satan worshipping goat fuckers anyway!"

They began to loosen up. I carried on.

"I'm not actually prepared for this. I only found out about it a few hours ago, so I'm going to wing it here and riff a little bit on writing."

A hand shot up.

"What is it damn it? I haven't even said anything yet!" I shouted.

"What would you say it takes to be a good writer?"

I could tell from his tone that he was a no good trouble maker.

"Well, let's see here. I think, to be considered a good writer in any sense, you must first have something to write about. That requires a certain amount of life experience, which you don't have because you don't look old enough to shave. Secondly, you need the capability to transmit that something through the written word. Both of these can generally take years to refine. And the competition in this field is brutal."

He raised his hand again and I nodded at this lost generation refugee. He was wearing a yellow striped cardigan – that meant danger. He was like a coiled cobra waiting to spring.

"What exactly do you mean when you say that the competition is brutal? I've never seen writing as *brutal*. Isn't it about *expressing* yourself?"

'Oh God,' I thought. 'He's got me by the balls!' I had to think on my feet.

"Well, it is about self-expression. But it's still a brutal field. When one considers the sheer number of books churned out by authors, regardless of quality, it is truly an astounding thing. This forms the basis of what becomes an aspiring writer's competition, because... in order for any writer to become a *success*, he or she has to tackle through those hordes and become noticed. It's like having the loudest voice in a room full of shouting children. That's how great writers like Hemingway, Fitzgerald and Twain did it. The key, however, isn't how many books you sell, poems you get published or even whether you please the critics. It comes down to whether you're happy with the quality of your work, and many young writers that are dismissed today may well become staples of literature in the future."

The oily slick snake sat there, unable to respond.

A roar of applause built up. I had absolutely no clue what the hell I was talking about. Matt got up, thanked me for my contribution and read some of Robert Burns' work as a follow up. I'd managed to get through the ordeal and left quietly before anyone noticed.

19. A Scientologist, An Evangelist
& A Page Three Girl With Herpes...

It was 7pm by the time I reached South Bridge. Drivers waited for the green at a set of temporary traffic lights while men with jackhammers ripped up the tarmac. I was glad to be away from the jungle-gym where well groomed gorillas thumped their chests in a show of verbal virility. The irony was that those hacks at the Forest lacked the fertile imagination necessary for the conception of new ideas. It wasn't their fault. They were born to be boring. I was not. But then, I'd subjected myself to too many extremes for prolonged periods of time. As any good psychologist will tell you, this generally results in a complete mental break from all known forms of reality.

While considering whether I was in fact experiencing one such episode, a man came toward me. I'd noticed him earlier in my peripheral vision, standing in a shady doorway where the light couldn't get to him. He extended his arm and grabbed my elbow with his free hand.

"My friend!" he said. "Aren't you sick of the way you're dictated to by the society and the media?"

"I suppose so," I replied.

"Well let me talk to you about a whole new wave of thinking, the way of the future!"

I didn't know this guy from Adam, yet already he'd called me his 'friend'. This troubled me. To throw the word around, like it meant nothing; as though friendships were something to be treated frivolously. It pissed me off. I preferred to remain his total stranger.

"Actually, I'd much rather not. I have a lot of stuff to do and..."

"Wait just a minute buddy!"

There it was again, this time disguised. How many 'buddies' did he have? Did I have cause to be jealous?

"This'll only take a few minutes of your time," he continued. "Our Academy offers free IQ tests... ah, I see you're a literary man."

I was carrying a leaflet from the café detailing its next poetry session.

"I wouldn't say that," I said.

"Well, did you know we offer lots of literature for free minds like yours?"

He was driving home the hard sell. His used car salesman slickness and clean cut appearance made me wary. You should never trust a man who looks better than you. Still, I did have some time to kill. My motto has always been 'if it's strange enough, jump in with both feet'.

"Tell me more," I said, grinning crazily.

He seemed a little stunned.

"I don't mind telling you, I've been standing here all day and you're the first person who's taken an interest. Why don't you come inside and I'll tell you all about it."

A big colourful sign was wedged above the doorway. I followed him and took a seat in what looked like a cheap imitation classroom. Formica covered desks and plastic moulded seats were sprawled across the visibly scratched laminate floor. He swirled round in high-back chair and began telling me how terrible things were.

"The government and news outlets use disinformation to control your mind, man! Have you ever noticed how the news is always designed to focus on the negative?"

This was true of course, but I was already aware of it.

"Well my friend, let me lay it on you and tell it like it is..."

It was then that he went on to expound the virtues of L. Ron Hubbard, a sci-fi author who'd written several books, mixing the ideas of Jung, Freud and Nietzsche with pseudo-scientific psycho babble. I'd read his Dianetics book. It was interesting and offered some unique ideas, but it wasn't a million miles from the ravings of Jim Jones – the preacher who'd engineered the Jonestown massacre.

He realised his slick pitch wasn't working and changed tactics.

"I'll tell you what, we'll give you one of our special intelligence tests and see how advanced you are in your evolution as a human being."

Who was 'we'? Up until then, it had been only him and me. Now it was apparent that our relationship wasn't going to be monogamous.

He dug out a printed sheet from his desk and gave it to me. I scanned through it briefly, scribbling away with a pencil he provided. I handed him the completed paper and walked over to the large panelled window. It seemed silly to be wasting my time indoors on a beautiful day. But I was getting a sick thrill from this cat and mouse game..

"Wow," he said as he marked the answers. "You're one smart guy!"

"I am?"

"Yeah, totally! You'd be a perfect candidate for joining us," he said.

"Well I don't know. I'm still not sure on that," I replied

"I have an idea. Why don't I show you some of our videos. I think you'd find them interesting. Then you can have a chat with one of our Auditors."

He escorted me to another room with a couch and a cheap DVD player. I watched a short twenty minute film that explained the freedom that was to be found in Scientology. They were careful not to call it a religion. I looked at the DVD case, part of a set that was priced at over a hundred pounds. You had to pay that if you wanted to be 'clear'. A 'clear' person was deemed to be at the highest level of personal wisdom. But you had to fork out some more dough before an 'auditor' confirmed your progress. By the end of it, you were either out of your mind or out of pocket, or maybe both.

In came the brown haired expert. Gone was the smiling face of my 'friend' who was 'hip' and 'down with it'. A piercing set of cold blue eyes took over, analysing my spiritual make-up from his supposedly elevated state of awareness. He recommended immediate induction. There was no time to lose. I was a suffering soul, doomed to an inner hell without the assistance of their program. It was imperative that I did what they told me, he explained.

"I'll need to think about it," I said.

"Why do you need to think about it?" he replied. "If you were diagnosed with cancer, would you need to *think* about treatment?"

The obvious answer was yes. But this freakish bastard was beginning to make me angrier with his analogy, citing a serious thing like cancer to sell me his wares. These were pressure tactics, plain and simple. The thickness of the bullshit was getting heavier and I no longer had the patience for his gibberish.

"You must listen to me!" he screamed. "I know what I'm talking about. You know nothing. I'm an expert. I've seen people like you refuse our help and it always ends in misery."

He couldn't have been older than twenty five. But here he was, with zero life experience, telling *me* that I was lacked sense.

"Listen you little piss ant," I shouted, "I've lived and learned more than your morally bankrupt soul will learn in ten lifetimes."

He didn't like that outburst very much and pressed a little green button on the wall. Three suits entered the room, grabbed me by the collar and threw me out. It was inevitable, but I'd hoped to get more of a debate from the fiendish little prick. Still, there was no real harm done and at least they hadn't taken it upon themselves to inflict a serious skull injury on my person. I went back on my way, safe in the knowledge that I'd soon be back on a train destined for Glasgow and I could put it all behind me. But this was not to be.

Near the Fruitmarket Gallery, I saw a young woman engaged in a battle of wits with a card-carrying conservative Christian. I recognised her from a newspaper clipping I'd come across last month. She was a glamour model who, as I recalled, had one of the finest female forms I'd seen in a while. Her favourite hobbies were chess and polo.

"Porn empowers people!" she screamed. "It leads to sexual, emotional and intellectual liberation. How dare you right wing nuts disempower women!"

"What *you* do is morally and socially repugnant!" he replied.

"People like you that can't see the inherent value of another human being. What concern is it of yours what women do with their bodies and sexuality?"

"Our country is saturated with porn and sexualised advertising in magazines. There's an epidemic of female eating disorders, self esteem issues and insecurity! Porn and page three are a great evil! So are the individuals in it, the sick freaks who look at it and the civilization that tolerates it!"

"And I'll bet you used to be one of them. Doesn't that make you 'evil' too?"

"The Lord has absolved me of all my sins. I have been

saved by the word. But you! You refuse to accept the truth. St Paul was right about women! It should be honour enough to bear our children and serve our needs. Why dishonour yourself and other women by doing things that will surely displease God?"

"What's wrong with you? Why do you fucking bible-thumpers always reduce us to non-beings, there to simply there to serve men? Throw out your outmoded ideas. There'd be no need for feminism if you just respected our decisions and gave us the equality, respect and love we deserve."

She was one clever cat. But so was the 'Jesus saves all' banner waving evangelist.

"What about having self-respect and not doing repulsive things for the love of money?"

It was then that I interjected.

"Dude, your views are obviously based on personal belief. You're coming from a place of moral absolutes, which is fine for people who are trapped in dogma…"

"I'm trapped in dogma? What about this porn obsessed society? It's everywhere brother!"

"We don't live in a 'pornographic' society; we live in a culture that's comfortable with itself. And as for eating disorders, it's sad when young boys and girls can't be happy with who they are. But that's *not* down to porn. It's to do with how people see themselves."

"And where does that come from man?"

"Well, it's usually rooted in the 'I hate myself' deep guilt complex that's espoused by the mainstream media, or religion even."

"Religion? You're blaming religion for it? How can you say that?"

"Well, sometimes the emphasis on sinning makes it hard for a person to love themselves."

"Jesus loves everyone."

"Maybe he does. But what happens to the people who don't do what God says?"

"They go hell."

"And he sends them there because he loves them?"

"Yes."

"I see."

"You're twisting my words! Haven't you seen the way provocative pictures have seeped into the world of advertising? It's all the doing of the adult industry man!"

"What the heck are you talking about? There's no goddamn link between sexualised advertising and porn. Advertising has always been about exploiting the less well off through mental indoctrination. Sure it's a bad thing. It's a form of brainwashing. No different to the constant references to hell and damnation in that book of yours."

"You heathen! How dare you!"

"Oh I dare alright. You see, sexual liberation teaches people to be free in themselves and their thinking. *Brainwashing* tells people *need* something, be it the fear of God, the latest trainers, or a car that will guarantee you hot chicks.

"So you don't think that flooding the minds of young men with filth is wrong and dangerous for their immortal souls?"

"No. In fact, it's probably healthy for them."

"Have you ever spent time in the company of a bunch of lads on the pull? They spend their developing years secretly jerking off to topless models. They ended up with a totally unrealistic view of their ideal woman and shun decent God-fearing women."

"If they're not rushing to wed church going girls, then trust me, it's not because of the adult industry. Has it occurred to you they just might not be into them? Everybody has their own type you know. Strong independent chicks are where it's at these days."

Miss June 12th nodded her head.

He turned to face her.

"You're naive and deluded, and should be ashamed of being in favour of an industry so destructive and debasing!"

For some reason that made me angry.

"There's the key word that your whole argument rests on – 'Ashamed' - Why should she feel 'ashamed' of *anything*? But yes, she *should* feel shame shouldn't she? So should *all* the women who have children outside of wedlock, gays, and people who don't put money into the collection plate every Sunday. If anyone's deluded it's a placard carrying freak who believes in an invisible man in the sky who tells him when to brush his teeth and will punish him in the fiery pits of Inferno if he doesn't do as he's told!"

He was silent for a few minutes and we both looked on as his face scrunched up as though he was being fingered by a fat nun.

"You're an atheist aren't you? I can tell. I pray for your lost soul. Because when you die, you're going to see that all the science in the world can't save you. You atheists just make up these facts and numbers!"

"Don't assume shit. You have no idea what I believe. Don't bother praying for me. You disguise insult as pity and expect me to accept that as some perverse form of Christ love? Fuck you man!"

"Your words don't affect me. Your science can't change the word of God!"

"Well, If you really want to get into the science versus religion debate, I'll kick your ignorant ass!"

"Try your best!" he hissed.

Like the biblical hero that was David, I was about to verbally slay this verbose fool and put the slimy bastard out of his misery. I cleared my throat and prepared to unleash an unparalleled onslaught. But he struck first.

"Can you prove that God doesn't exist? Can't you see his wonders around you?" he asked.

"If you mean God as in the wonder of life then you're being metaphorical. But we can't forget the harsh brutality of nature. There are birth defects, pathogens, parasites and so on that you creationist bozos utterly ignore."

"But belief had to originate somewhere! People wouldn't have started believing in God if he didn't exist," he replied.

"Well," I said. "Many stories and legends exist in plenty of cultures. They evolved from exaggerated claims about someone or something they saw. Like the Sun. There were lots of Sun gods in a lot of religions."

He thought about this for a moment before retorting.

"But Christianity is the only religion that gives us answers. It helps people make sense of the world by giving them the right moral codes to live by."

"To make sense of the world, it's not in some divine book that we need to look, but outside at the greater picture; that's where true miracles exist."

"What do you mean?" he asked.

"Those of us that are happy and healthy have, by the laws of probability, beaten the odds. I'd say that's the real miracle. And as social animals, we should ensure that the ones who didn't survive the battle unscathed, are looked after better and not preyed upon by charlatans and power mad institutions."

He looked on as he listened to the ravings of a caffeine crazed insomniac. Still though, he tried to go against the grain of common sense.

"Yes, but science and rationality can't give people the things religion can. People like you aggressively preach science as if it can replace the Ten Commandments."

"Science and religion are not and cannot be on the same footing. Religiously motivated types like you seem to say that Science itself is a belief. It isn't. It is the reasoned application of logic and method to a series of hypothesis which can be falsified.

"Ah, so you're saying that science can be based on falsehoods!"

"No, you moron! The word means that science is an open field, using what can be proven are its guiding force. Religion, in any faith base, is absolute in its conclusions. When evidence contradicts its ideals, it tries to adapt, but can't."

"But scientists do make stuff up. Look at all the theories out there. They're just ideas that are being taught as true!"

"Oy vey! Did you not go to school? The definition of a scientific theory is that it's a proven hypothesis, with hard facts to back it up. A theory is the highest achievement in any scientific field. So science does not simply 'make things up'."

"Ah, so you're Jewish! You should know better. You do know that if you die, you're going to hell, don't you?" he said.

"Oh, my dear idiotic friend! There is no hell but what we make. If there was, and your God was that unmerciful, then I'd happily go there. I wouldn't want to be blessed by a vengeful god who hears the screams of hungry children in Africa and ignores them."

"It's all a test!" he replied, now aggravated.

"A test?" I asked. "A test for who?"

"For us. For people who can do something about it."

"So, let me get this straight. Your God makes innocent people suffer to test your beliefs? That doesn't sound very loving."

By now he'd worked himself into a fanatical frenzy.

"Your souls are damned! Especially this whore's!" he screamed.

"Shut the fuck up you zealot! People like you kill Jesus everyday by preaching this crap. And I can tell you voted for Tony Blair. May God have mercy on your shit-filled brain!"

Miss June 12th stood there open mouthed, obviously not expecting some whacked out stranger to leap to her defence in this way. The man with the placard stood there, stumped and silent.

"May God give you both herpes!" he yelled.

"I've already had it!" giggled the girl.

I resumed my journey toward Waverly station. She skipped up alongside me in her boob tube and black miniskirt. Her curly blonde hair gave her an almost angelic glow.

"Thanks for what you did back there. You didn't have to do it. It was really sweet."

"It was nothing. It's just been one of those days. I'd had enough of crazy fuckers and their nonsense. I can't stand folk who think they can push people around."

"My name's Tina. I guess you already know what I do for a living. I'm sorry people had to see that."

"Don't be sorry. What are you gonna do? Let that kind of behaviour slide? Better to call them on it."

"Yeah. You're right," she said. "I never caught your name?"

"My name's Max," I replied.

"Where ya from? You don't sound like you're from Edinburgh."

"I'm not. I'm a Weegie. Not born in Glasgow, but definitely bred there. You?"

"I'm from Hamilton originally."

"Ah, Hamilton. The place where undead souls beckon Glaswegians with sweet promises of Buckfast and unabashed glue sniffing orgies. No mortal can resist, save the few who know the holy words... 'C'mone then ya bam!'"

She laughed.

"You're a weird and funny guy. I like your style Max. You heading back to Glasgow?"

"Yeah, that was the plan. I only came down for a fundraiser at the Forest Café. "

"Sounds like fun."

"It wasn't."

"Mind if I come with you? I was planning in going into Glasgow anyway. My parents stay there. I could use some good company on the journey down. I'll be on my best behaviour. I promise not to start any more public riots!"

We walked together the rest of the way back to Waverley. She spoke a lot. I wasn't sure if she was just nervous or hyper. Either way, she seemed like a nice girl. She sat next to me in the last compartment of the train. Tina talked about her family, her sisters and her parents who had been very supportive of her life choices. I was a little envious. I'd never had that kind of family security. I didn't say much. I kept her amused with some funny stories. The train rocked back and forth and put us both to sleep. Her head fell onto my shoulder and I let her rest against it. Other people got on while the driver remained ever vigilant in heralding each stop.

20. Nymphet Joyriders From Mars...
The Secret Sex-Tapes Of Wallis Simpson...

We pulled into Queen Street station at around 10.45pm. Tina lifted her head from my shoulder. My arm had fallen asleep and the sleeve of my turtleneck was covered in drool. I was mildly irritated, but her soft green eyes made it difficult to be mad at her. There was only one other person in the carriage. He was busy tapping away on his iPhone, oblivious to the world outside his techno bubble. It was turning dark and an orange glow hovered over the night sky. Tina fumbled with her skirt. Perhaps she felt a chill. Or maybe some semblance of modesty had infiltrated her unabashed personality.

"Listen, let me give you my number," she said.

"Oh okay. Sure."

"Well... I don't have any business cards on me or anything..."

That much was evident. It would have been difficult to conceal a stack of cards anywhere in that get-up.

"Do you have a pen?"

I riffled through my trouser pocket and pulled out a miniature pen that doubled as a cigarette lighter. I'd bought it at a gadget store and had only used it once in four years.

"Thanks. You don't have any paper do you?"

I checked. I didn't.

"Afraid not."

"That's okay. Hold out your hand."

She scribbled on my right palm and I watched as the ink marked my leathery skin.

"Now, don't wash it off until you get a chance to write it down! I really do want you to give me a call sometime."

We walked together toward the exit. It occurred to me that

there wasn't a ticket inspector aboard the train. Not even the man at the turnstiles had asked us to show him one. Tina had bagged herself a free ride. She was beginning to grow on me. But that quip about herpes made me uneasy.

There was a row of black cabs waiting outside the station. She flagged the first and I climbed into the one behind. On the way home I felt a profound sense of calm. I wasn't sure if it was the drive or just the encounter with a beautiful girl. I had no plans to call her. She'd understand. She was after all a woman of the world; she knew damn well how the game was played. In the frenetic field of hook-ups, you either played for sport or were in it to win it; the brass ring. I'd once enjoyed he thrill of the chase and the joy of sexual conquest, but it was no longer enough. I wanted something more, needed it too much. That was probably the thing that hit me in the balls in all my relationships. The dreaded curse of a hungry heart.

I remembered the advice of a friend who once said that 'all relationships, friendships and other ships go through rough seas.' But some are doomed from the start, like the Titanic. In the 21st Century, nothing was certain. You could rely on no-one. It was ultimately always better to keep your own counsel. Trust no-one; at least not entirely.

"That's nine quid and sixty mate," said the cab driver.

I panicked for a moment, thinking that I'd left my wallet on the train, but I found it in my back pocket, bent out of shape. I'd been sitting on it for the better part of ninety minutes. I took out my last twenty and handed it to him, counting the change he returned carefully. When you're facing financial ruin, every penny matters.

I was glad to be back in my nest again. The light in the landing wasn't working and it made it that much harder to grapple with the key. I locked the door and kicked off my shoes. My answering machine was beeping. I didn't want to be disturbed by anything and I debated whether or not to bother checking my messages. But I got up anyway and clicked the replay button.

"Max? Its Rollie. My PC isn't working. I was wondering if you had a spare laptop I could borrow? Anyway, call me back when you get in."

Rollie was one of my best friends. He was a Welsh/English German Jew by descent. He'd been part of the 60's free speech explosion and had lived to tell the tale. When the whole hippy movement collapsed, he escaped its madness and moved north. He married and settled in a tranquil part of Glasgow. That was before his wife left him literally holding the baby. He'd single-handedly fulfilled his paternal responsibilities and worked full-time. He reminded me of someone. Aside from this, he was also a prominent figure in the underground arts community, dabbling in everything from painting to photography. But all this made the man as unhinged as I was. It would be true to say that he'd become a father figure who I looked up to. He'd recently shacked up with a marvellous broad who generally kept him on the straight and narrow.

I dialled his number on the retro telephone on my desk. It rung out for a while before he finally answered. He was clearly sloshed out of his skull.

"Rollie? It's Max. I got your message."

"Ah yes dear boy. Glad you called. The missus and I were just discussing the merits of modern technology."

"I see. What happened to the computer?"

"Well. How can I put this? It took over three minutes to load. So I smashed it to smithereens with that sledgehammer in the tool shed."

"Did that help? They do say that sometimes all you need to do is give it a good thump."

"Well no. It stopped working completely. You know what the sad thing is?"

"What?" I asked

"I was in the middle of downloading that smut collection for you. You remember the one we were talking about?"

"Smut collection? Oh you mean the 'Fat Nymphet Joyriders From Mars' special edition box set!"

"That's the one!" he said.

"That's terrible. Absolutely terrible. You know my life is empty without a bit of alien sex to spice it up. I'm already suffering from withdrawal symptoms man! I'm growing hair on my palms and my vision goes wonky every Saturday night!"

"You may have to resort to calling the Russell Grant's psychic sex line for depraved addicts - approved and funded by the generous contributions of Clegg & Cameron."

"My God! I don't want to have to resort to that kind of lowlife debasement. Isn't there anything you can do?"

"Well. I did find a mint copy of anal boys in lederhosen. It's a Nazi special starring Himmler and a thousand brown shirts."

"Wow. Is that even... legal? I mean I've heard the stories, but man it's supposedly *so* hardcore that even the Duchess of York squealed in terror after seeing it. I must have it!"

"Did you hear? Wallis Simpson is in the last reel. She's the one with the jellyfish. It's yours for two pounds of mackerel and a steel penis enhancer. Viagra just isn't doing it for me anymore."

"Blimey! I think I can arrange that. Ah, Wallis Simpson. The poor man's answer to Winifred Wagner. And with a jellyfish too eh? Yes, yes, yes! You will have your enhancer; but the mackerel may be a problem. I already gave three pounds of it to the Tory fund for free enemas."

"The Tories get free enemas? Damn that's news to me!"

"Tell me about it! Shocking isn't it?"

"Max, this conversation has probably gone past any bounds of dignified discourse. The missus is giving me strange looks of disapproval."

"So, this computer thing. Yes, you can have my spare laptop if you need it. It's fifteen years old and I haven't used it lately so I can't promise that it's working."

"Thanks. It's better than nothing. I just need it to write up some basic stuff and surf the internet a little. Does it have a word processor and wireless capability?"

"Yeah. It should have. I'll drop it by in a couple of days."

"Great. By the way, how was America?"

"It was good. Still where I left it."

"Glad you're back young man. Anyway, thanks again. Take care for now."

Rollie had kept up with all the latest techno fads and was more in tune with them than most young people.

I contemplated the marvels of the internet age. All information was now digitised, consumed as raw data. It was an awesome leap of human innovation. No-one in their wildest dreams could have imagined such things, not even in Rollie's age of inspiration. But with it came inherent dangers. It was all too easy for some all powerful force to make anything unfavourable vanish by simply pressing the 'delete' button. We were already seeing the beginnings of this phenomenon in certain forums. Even with things like 'Facebook', 'Youtube' and 'Myspace', which were frequently totted out as being bastions of freedom, platforms for self-expression.

We were close to a time when we wouldn't need things like newspapers or paper of any sort. There would be no recorded interviews, no written records, no hardcopy to fall back on. Issues like Iraq's WMD scandal, the death of Dr David Kelly and ongoing foreign invasions couldn't be probed and analysed by the vigilant public. No unforeseen problems could topple governments or tackle injustice with legitimacy.

I wondered if Orwell's nightmare was coming true. The future map for the digital age pointed to a path paved with good intentions, great sound bites and free junk content for all; a yellow brick road laden with gold for the toll-masters. But its final destination was probably somewhere far too shocking for us to contemplate.

The government had vowed to tackle what it called 'declining morality' among the young people of today. The student protests and other incidents had disturbed the rich fat cats so much that they were now prepared to go all Clockwork Orange on them. And then they wondered *why* people kept saying that they were out of touch.

It was past midnight. I switched on the television and flicked over to the twenty-four hour news channel to catch up on two days worth of headlines. In the early hours of the 5th of August 2011, £125billion had been wiped off share prices and the value of the FTSE100 had fallen by more than 8%, a 12 month low. 'More than £1.2trillion erased in share value globally'. The ticker at the bottom of the screen kept scrolling. How could I have missed this?

World markets were collapsing and I'd been busy partying. It was probably just as well. There wasn't much else to do except storm the streets in a fear driven frenzy. But that would accomplish nothing and only result in mass panic. Governments across the globe knew that. That was why, for three years, they had been reluctant to admit to the real extent of the financial problem, and it was spreading like wildfire, infecting every economy. At first it was just a slow down. Then it was stagnation. In a matter of months, it was a recession. No-one had yet dared to use the proper word for it - Depression.

As usual, the people at the top weren't going to be affected. Banks and their top employees were still being paid obscene bonuses, despite having created the problem. Politicians were also raking it in while making cuts to wages and hiking up taxes. "We have a strategy," they kept saying. "We're in this together!"

It's a commonly accepted belief that no-one in politics will ever tell the truth. And it was out there now, ugly and naked. There was no solution. The brakes had failed, the wheels had come off and we had a runaway that was going to crash and burn. Like any out of control locomotive, it presents a threat to anyone crossing the tracks.

But this was no concern of mine; for the simple reason that we had gone beyond the point of no return. We passed that point fifty years ago, when banking cartels and government institutions colluded to allow financiers to value all national assets and currency through centralised banking, and boy did they rack up those debts beyond calculable sums.

Yet it would be equally right to say that all was not lost. None of the great disasters in human history had wiped us out as a species. All it would take was a handful of intellectuals who could think outside the box. If they examined it logically, people would quickly realise that just as we'd created the entire system out of thin air, we could make it vanish through collective acceptance. It *was* all an illusion from start to finish.

However, this is not an easy thing for your average sane person to accept. Sane people can only handle increments of spoon-fed information. No rational human being *wants* to think for themselves. It takes up too much valuable time and effort, amd as we'd all been harshly brainwashed into believing, time is money. That's why the internet provided pan-handled bite sized chunks of content; fast geared spokes turning the thumbscrews in a computerised domain.

I switched channels and caught the end of the Jeremy Kyle Show. The topic was alcoholism, which he kept referring to as a 'disease'. Cancer was a disease, Chlamydia was a disease. Alcoholism was a desire; a need that burned through your liver and into the soft squishy part of your brain. You lusted for it; ached for it; until you felt it coursing through your every vein and artery.

Viewing trash TV always made me thirsty. I scooped out some ice-cubes from the freezer and popped them into a small tumbler filled with Southern Comfort. I could hear the ice crack as it soaked up the liquor. It had been an eventful but tiring day. I gulped down the sweet liquid and reloaded.

I flicked through the newspaper I'd bought the previous day. The most interesting story, apart from the phone hacking scandal, was President Barrack Obama's fiftieth birthday. Jennifer Hudson was signed up and set to sing at the Aragon Ballroom for the big bash. He was said to be looking forward to the festivities, despite having just dodged the bullet on the agreement to raise the debt ceiling, which could have led to the first default in American history.

The plight of hungry children in Sudan was given little more than a small caption at the bottom of the eighth page. The war torn region of Darfur was being ripped apart by armed conflict, kids were losing their lives and limbs. But the biggest thing that we had to worry about in the west was money; earned from selling the same arms that and blew theirs off. You couldn't make it up. The more you saw of it, the sicker it made you.

In these dragon ridden years, if you started out mentally balanced, the chances were that you'd end up bat-shit crazy by the end. In all the millennia we'd spent on this planet, we hadn't outgrown our desire to kill each other. Here we were, floating through the cosmos, fucking up almost everything we got our grubby human hands on.

By three o'clock I was sufficiently drunk enough not to be pained by the awfulness of the truth. The room started spinning. I heard a distant voice shrieking and sobbing in fits of uncontrollable rage. No doubt another desperado lamenting his existence on this earthly plane.

21. Keys To The Kingdom...
United We Fall...

After 48 hours of intravenously injecting Southern Comfort into my system I was still alive. It was an encouraging sign. They say you should treat your body like a temple and I did, regularly cleansing it with alcohol. But I would need a bucket full of Aspirin, a defibrillator and a possible brain transplant to lift me out of my comatose state this time. I didn't want to get up. My throat was dry and an unhealthy cough erupted from my lungs. Catarrh shot up like froth inside a cappuccino maker. I spent the next twelve or so minutes hacking violently in the bathroom and another ten shitting a never-ending stream of liquefied manure. Had I contracted some deadly disease? Perhaps it was Fijian flatulence fever; my doctor's surgery was littered with leaflets on dangerous tropical infections.

Finally, I regained control of my bowels. I thought about making some toast; but then I remembered that my toaster had been stolen. The fridge was virtually empty, except for three oranges, a brown banana and a red apple. A fruit salad seemed the best option. I threw some clothes into the washing machine. It was an old model and both its feet were damaged. It danced around, jumping off the linoleum like James Brown. Fortunately, the water hose was long enough to avoid the risk of flooding. The lady downstairs frequently complained about it. "Tenants like you should be shot!" she screamed.

I didn't have the money to replace it. Besides, it made laundry day all the more exciting. A couple of years back, an ex girlfriend wanted to have sex on top of it. It was as uncomfortable as riding a bronco in a Texas rodeo. But she was addicted. Eventually, fearing serious injury, I decided to end it. They were fond memories.

I grabbed a small knife from the cutlery drawer. The banana and apple were easy to cut up, but the logistics of trying to chop an orange into solid chunks proved difficult. A nutritious breakfast was the cornerstone of a healthy lifestyle and I was a picture of perfect health; the poster-child for the recommended five a day. I took a swig of whiskey.

It was late in the afternoon when I stopped in at the corner store. I had just enough for a pack of cigarettes, some gum and a newspaper. The pot-bellied Sikh owner was always grateful for my custom. He greeted me in his usual cheery manner. We spoke for a short while about the dreadful state of the economy. He seemed confident that it would pass quickly. I was not so sure. I paid him and left.

I glanced at the front page and let out a whimper after reading the headline. Mass riots had broken out across London. It started in Brixton after police officers shot and killed a young black man. Mark Duggan died on the 4th of August and by the 6th chaos was sweeping the city.

It was inevitable. The police were quickly becoming a law unto themselves. Stop and search powers had been increased, the right to free speech had been curbed and people were being singled out as a result of racial profiling. They – the police - were beyond reproach. The death of Ian Tomlinson had already demonstrated that. Even when all the evidence pointed to them being in the wrong, they somehow managed to cover each others backs.

Usually when the powers that be decreed something, we quietly grumbled and accepted it. But something was different here. What had given people in London such a kick in the balls that they felt violent anarchy was the only answer?

It came down to a simple matter of truth and dishonesty. The police had released statements implying that Mr Duggan had fired at officers with a gun, forcing them to shoot him dead. The family maintained that it was outside the boy's character. On the 6th, they held what started out as a peaceful protest, asking only for an accurate account of events that led to the tragedy. Around two-hundred people gathered to join them, demanding to speak directly to a senior officer. Their demands were not met. The situation escalated as more people joined the righteous cause. But a few troublemakers were carrying weapons. Clashes between the police and the agitators followed and rioting and looting quickly took hold. Random acts of destruction became the language of an unheard people, angry about the way the system kept crushing them under its weight. Arson and intimidation were the verbs they used to get their point across. Was their behaviour excusable? Absolutely. However, the problem with anarchy is that it doesn't have a defined target. The law abiding public, who are themselves victims, get caught in the crossfire.

Any original purpose got pulped by the angry masses baying for blood. Just who or what they were attacking remained unclear. What was becoming clear was that they were now running loose, untamed and feral, like a pack of dingoes, searching for nothing more than devastation as an end in itself.

Fear is a dangerous thing. People did a lot of stupid things out of fear; or didn't do the things they should have. Courage and strength make life worth living. No-one should settle for less. But in this case, the police were afraid, the rioters were afraid and neither side was prepared for the consequences of their respective actions.

That evening I watched the carnage unfold as live footage was transmitted to a frightened nation. The leaders of the country were nowhere to be found, sunning themselves on sandy beaches on their all expenses paid vacations, funded by the taxpayer. The riots were spreading beyond London's city limits. Birmingham,

Nottingham, Leicester, West Bromwich, Wolverhampton, Bury, Liverpool, Manchester, Rochdale, Salford, Sefton and even Wirral; the list was ever growing, cities ablaze in the fires of disenchanted youth.

The looting and pillaging reminded me of all the fun times of my own formative years. The sad truth was that these people had no future to look forward to, and no other outlet for their frustrations. They'd descended to the level of inhuman beasts. I knew about this from my own experiences. All they *really* needed were adults who give a fuck about where they were at 2am on a school night, and a chance at a decent education that could lead toward a constructive life. These things were being taken away from them by the government's austerity measures. Parents couldn't focus on their children because they were busy breaking their backs for bread, teachers in classrooms couldn't teach because their resources were shrinking and the jobs market was saturated with overqualified applicants struggling with the haunting spectre of unemployment.

When statements were finally made by our fearful leaders, they said it was imperative that the state come down hard on those responsible for this loutish behaviour. It was 'terrorising' the good people of the United Kingdom. They would outlaw this 'criminality'. Their own, particularly during the expenses scandal, was of no consequence. These bastard youth had to be caught and caged for the remainder of their natural lives. This seemed a reasonable course of action. After all, no sane human being would advocate this kind of heinous behaviour. They were turning entire cities upside down.

Justice was a joke. We all knew that the great lady had been stripped of her blindfold and whored to her rich overlords. They were the only ones who could afford her. By Vatican standards, she was an unclean harlot. This was the British

Nightmare in all its glory. Divided we stand, united we fall: one nation under law enforcement.

There was only so much a man could take before these terrible scenes shattered his soul. In all the noise and panic, people had entirely forgotten about the real victims, who'd lost their son to a sequence of miscalculations and exaggerated half-truths. The relatives of Mark Duggan would feel their loss forevermore.

Malcolm X once said, "I have no mercy or compassion in me for a system that will crush people and penalise them for not being able to stand up under the weight."

It was as true today as it was in his day. The Duggan family had come under the wheels of a rigid machine that championed deceit. The sheer amount of skull-fuckery in this world knew no bounds. Birds did it, bees did it, authorities did it and even the PM did it. Was any room left for straight-talking men of moral character?

I switched off the television but I couldn't get the images out of my mind; they were stuck there, like a love-child borne from the loins of Tony Blair and Barbara Bush. You know you don't want it to be real; you keep hoping that you'll wake up and find out that it was all just a horrible dream. But sadly, the bastard reality was there in front of you. It had to be dealt with. This was not something our trusted leaders did well. They were not used to seeing things as they were; they were used to seeing things that never were and convincing themselves that they were right.

Meanwhile, the very fabric of our society was disintegrating. Something had to be done. But no-one could say what. No half-measures were going to work. The only sure way to fix the engine was to rip out its guts, re-invent it and replace every rusty cog that had clogged it up with sticky-fingered thievery and empty promises. Everywhere you looked the cloak of darkness was draped around an infernal figure, crooked as the u-bend of a blocked toilet and just as eager to erupt sewage over the unstained population.

My cerebral cortex was overloaded with dismal undertones that pierced my inner bubble of calmness. I was too rattled and hung-over to cope with the full extent of the events that were transpiring. Below the belt punches where coming from all directions, with a speed not seen since the Boxing bouts of Muhammad Ali, and the whole country was feeling it. We just weren't ready for the kind of demented activity that was sweeping the land.

I couldn't sit there lamenting the state of the nation. It was too far gone to be saved. No method of CPR could bring it back from the brink. It was taking its last dying breaths. The interesting thing about the death of a country is that it conforms to the Buddhist idea symbolised by the Ouroboros – the image of a snake eating its own tail. It represents the circle of life. Death to rebirth.

I didn't really feel like spending another day by myself. Especially with everything that was going on. Rollie would be home by now. I'd told him I'd bring over the laptop and that moment seemed as good a time as any. The computer bag was stuffed in my closet. I opened it up and examined the contents carefully. The computer whirred as I hit the power button and it went through the motions, displaying a welcome screen proudly across its 14inch monitor. It was in working condition alright. I shut it down and packed it up.

It was 8pm. Time had just frittered away. It was a curious thing, time. Some days seemed unending, some passed so fast you barely recall where they started. There were even weeks that merged from one to the next.

Buses were running a Sunday service. I called the taxi

company. The lady on the other end made idle conversation while she radioed it through.

"Have you heard the news?" she asked. "Isn't it just awful? I've got relatives down there. I'm so worried."

"Yes, it's terrible," I said.

She sensed that I didn't want to talk about it.

When I got to Rollie's two large garbage bins were blocking the entrance to the close. They were empty. I moved them to the side of the door and rang the bell. 'Help me Rhonda' echoed through the building.

"What!" screamed the voice on the intercom.

"Rollie you old bastard, open the damned door you degenerate! It's me."

"Max? Yes of course. Come on up!"

Rollie lived three stories up. I never looked forward to tackling the never-ending series of stairs. He'd chosen to live there on purpose, thinking that it would help keep his heart healthy and increase his fertility. I was always surprised by his ability to leap over small steps in a single bound. He was fitter than I was and had the arteries of a twelve year old. My own, on the other hand, were clogged with stale cigarettes and thick buttered rolls.

There on his sofa sat Trisha Patterson. Trisha was a curvaceous and beautiful young woman, as full bodied as a good wine. I drank in her image while she rolled a joint on a Rolling Stones vinyl cover. Her strawberry blonde hair stopped just past her shoulders. I'd never managed to muster the words to ask her out. The furthest I'd gotten was some lame line about how great she looked in red.

I handed Rollie the laptop. He was in no rush to test it and offered me a glass of Glenmorangie. The TV was on in the background but Rollie had turned the sound off. Gina, his other half, came through from the study. They'd been going steady for a while. Everyone talked about how the two seemed made for each other. I was glad for Rollie, but a part of me felt a sense of sadness at never having experienced that sort of love. I'd long ago come to the conclusion that a man like me was destined never to find it.

The single malt went down smoothly and I helped myself to another dram whilst total coverage of the riots was broadcast on TV. We lowered our heads, unwittingly synchronous, unable to bring ourselves to say anything. Rollie was never lost for words, but even he knew that on this occasion, there was nothing that would take away from the unbelievable awfulness of it all. There was only one thing to do; deny it was actually happening. Trisha was the first to speak.

"They shouldn't have shot that wee boy in the first place. That wasn't right how he died. He didn't have to die."

She was right. There was no reason why this vile chain of events had to happen. All it would have taken was some rational thought from the authorities and they would have realised that honesty was the best policy. But the sad truth was, we'd become so accustomed to lying that it was the only thing we expected anymore from anyone.

"Trish, you know better than anyone, life isn't fair. Good people die, bad people prosper. There's no method in the madness. It's like you say about how animals get slaughtered by the billions for the sake of corporate greed. It's no different when it comes to our own kind. We suck as a species," I said.

Trisha was a child of the 70's, raised by hippy generation parents stuck in the 60's. She was an avid environmentalist and vegan. Trish had big tits and a bigger mind. Her heart? The biggest. She'd seen a lot in her life, coping with most of it, hurting from some of it and managed to come out the other end stronger. She was about the most normal human being I knew. Normal, but by no means boring. She had a lot to say on a whole number of things. We'd argued many a time over opposing views on a range of things, including my man-crush on Hemingway (who she felt was a misogynist) to my daily meat-eating orgies. It was safe to say I liked her a lot. But a decent girl like that would never take interest in a certifiable lunatic like me.

"Yeah. I know, but don't you just wish sometimes that life would cut us all some slack? I mean none of us asked to be here. You'd think we'd have developed the smarts to know not to kill each other."

"That's true," said Gina. "Rollie and I were talking about this just yesterday. All the wars. There's been so many for no good reason. World War I, World War II, Korea, Vietnam, Iraq, Afghanistan and now Libya."

Rollie added his two cents worth.

"Yes, but darling, you're forgetting one thing. There's a very good reason behind them all: profit. We, the British Government, make a lot of money selling arms to both sides in any armed conflict. Then of course there's the construction contracts and oil contracts and all sorts of deliciously devious things that bring in the dough."

I couldn't fault his logic. He was right about the wars. Except this was different. This wasn't about war or making money. This was full throttle lawlessness brought about by errors in judgement. There was nothing to be gained from any of it on either side.

"But these riots Rollie, they're not profiting anyone."

"Are you sure about that Max?" he said. "The looting *is* about money, the lack of it at least; the haves being targeted by the have nots."

22. The Terrifying Formless Shape of Tomorrow's Child...

"Well, they're certainly sowing the seeds of their own demise," I said. "Do you remember the student protests last year? That kid on a wheelchair got dragged across the street and beaten by the cops. Every time they step over the mark, they keep expecting nothing to happen. This time something happened."

"Yeah. I almost wish I was with the rioters," said Rollie.

"We're too old for that sort of thing. It's a game for cocky young roosters with iPods who've stared at the jowls of Theresa May's crank addled face and lived to tell the tale. None of that horror for us matey. You won't catch us stealing toilet seats and Alba TVs," I said.

"If things don't cool off, they'll mobilise every policeman in Britain and they'll come down on them like a ton of bricks!" added Gina.

"Aye. We're in a right sorry state. Thank goodness nothing like that's happened up here in Scotland," said Trisha.

"Never say never," I said. "All that trouble could easily head up here if someone stirred us up."

Trisha lit up the spliff and passed it around. I took a good few puffs to calm my rattled nerves. Rollie picked up the Rolling Stones album sitting on the arm of the couch.

"Shall I put this on? Better than watching that mind numbing drivel on the news."

We all nodded. Unlike me, when Rollie got angry over something, he'd become very quiet and stand there squinting at some unseen force in the ether, squeezing his fist until all the blood drained from his knuckles. I could tell he was quickly reaching this point when I saw all four fingers curl into his hand. It wouldn't take much to send Rollie over the edge. He was one of those hardcore believers who didn't just dangle their legs over the precipice; they threw themselves down the cliff, with all the intensity of a 747 jumbo jet.

He lined up the LP on the record player and set the needle on the first track, 'Sympathy for the Devil'. Mick Jagger's vocals screeched at us in tinny tones and we sang along. It wasn't really singing, it was more of a rabble, the combined out of tune attempts at trying to drown out the negative vibrations that had infiltrated our spirits. We were in freefall, musical notes bouncing off the walls. Trisha's aura turned wild, fiery red and her arms were up in the air, saluting the Mongolian sky god Tengri. Gina got up and danced against Rollie in a riled sexual manner, not wanting to waste his potent angry energy.

I swayed my head to the beat for a while before giving up on any hope of getting up. I was too mellow and didn't particularly want to change that. I opened a bottle of rum I'd stolen from Rollie's fridge and drank some more. Trisha was making eyes at me from across the room. The hi-fi scratched and crackled as it hit the end of the record. The three took a break and plopped down onto the beige sofa. Rollie and Gina cooed to each other in a sickening display of affection.

"Pass us the bucket!" said Trisha.

"I'll second that!" I said.

"What do you think missus? Shall we continue torturing these silly sausages?" said Rollie.

"Well guys, I'll let you two love birds get an early night," I said.

"No, stay my friend. We're not at all sleepy and we do so enjoy your company," said Rollie.

"Who said anything about sleep?" I said, winking at Gina.

"Enjoy yourselves you crazy kids!"

"How will you get home at this hour?" asked Gina.

She had a point. It was eleven thirty and there was no hope

of catching a bus on a Sunday night at this hour.

"I'll cab it as usual," I said.

"Listen, you're welcome to crash here Max. I'll share a secret. This couch isn't just a couch. It's a sofa-bed!" said Rollie.

"That's very James Bond of you," I replied. "But I really should get home. Besides, isn't Trish crashing here too? There's not enough space here for you to have two guests staying over."

"We can both take the sofa-bed. It's not a good idea for you to be alone when you're this drunk," said Trisha.

She seemed genuinely concerned about my well-being. But I wasn't overly inebriated and I'd been in much worse shape many a time. Still, I felt rather comfortable at Rollie's and didn't really want to go back to an empty flat.

"Well, alright," I said. "I'll take that offer. I appreciate it."

"No problem young man. It's our pleasure to have you over. Now if you'll excuse us, me and the missus are going to retire for the evening. You and Trish make yourselves at home. There's blankets and bedding in the airing cupboard."

With Trisha's help I folded out the sofa-bed and grabbed a couple of pillows and some sheets from the cupboard.

"You prefer a side?" I asked Trisha.

"I don't mind. You?"

"I'll take the right. I prefer being next to the window. Probably sounds silly but I like being able to see the sky," I said.

She smirked and fired a pillow at my chest. I caught it before it hit the ground and placed it at the head of the spongy mattress. I laid down on the outer edge and Trisha took the left side, with an imaginary boundary line dividing us according to ancient rules of Victorian propriety. The truth was I was ill at ease in the company of a beautiful woman who I harboured deep and lascivious feelings for. Whether the horror of the day's events added to my anxiety, or whether it was the awful gut-wrenching pain of what I'd gone through with Kandy, I couldn't say. But whatever it was, I'd no sooner drifted off than I found Trisha shaking me awake and hovering over me.

"Max! Max!"

"Jesus! God Almighty! What the hell is it?" I shouted.

"Oh my God, you worried the hell out of me. You were talking and crying in your sleep. Thank God you're okay."

"I was?" I said. I felt the cold sweat dripping down my back. "Sorry. It happens sometimes. I hope it didn't scare you."

"Nightmare?" she asked.

"Night-terrors," I replied.

"Oh," she said. "You should see someone about that."

"Yeah," I said. "Haven't had them since I was a child."

Her voice calmed my shaky disposition and her soothing gentleness eased my troubled soul. She held me tightly in her arms and my hand reached out to meet hers. It was as if Mother Mary had descended from heaven itself to answer my silent prayers. My inner animal was tamed; dormant; unable to claw its way out of the barren wasteland it had thrived in for so long. It didn't want to feed. It didn't want to fuck. It was rendered useless in the presence of this beautiful creature. Her head rested on my chest.

"I can feel your heart-beat," she said.

We both lost ourselves in a mist of dreams, happy and high. I got up sometime around noon. Trisha was nowhere to be seen. Rollie had made brunch; French toast, poached eggs and salmon, along with a cup of Earl Grey. The plate on the coffee table was still warm. I stacked away the bedding back in the airing cupboard and folded up the sofa-bed. Gina strolled in, clad in a pink dressing gown.

"Glad to see you're up," she said. "Rollie's in the study putting the finishing touches on his latest painting. I know he'd love your opinion on it."

"Oh okay," I replied. "Did Trish leave?"

"Yeah. She's rehearsing for that new play. Ah, the glamorous life of an actor!" she chuckled.

I was slightly disappointed, but also glad in a way. With daylight came a self-confidence that was not to be found in the darkness of night. I hurriedly ate breakfast from Rollie's best china. Gina switched on the TV. On the extended one o'clock news bulletin, they were discussing the aftermath of the recent wave of 'criminality'. There was that word again. There were no reported deaths, just a great deal of vandalism. I was sure that the powers that be were secretly conducting nightly rituals, sacrificing virgins to giant statues of Moloch, hoping that they could pin a few murder raps on some of the offenders. That would give them a blank check for a ban on bedlam of any kind.

I took my tea to Rollie's study and knocked on the door three times in a coded sequence that only retired 33rd degree Freemasons could understand.

"Abandon all hope if you're going to enter!" roared a voice.

I stared at the fine crafted brushwork on the canvas. Flaming embers of red danced around burning buildings and bullet-proof shields. A blurred shapeless face stood in the middle, gagged with a Union Jack flag.

"Well? What do you think?" asked Rollie.

"It's... Interesting," I said.

"Interesting? Just interesting?" he screeched. "I spent three weeks on this thing!"

"I mean its bloody fantastic!"

"But?"

"But I'm not entirely sure the world of British art is ready for this sort of thing," I replied.

"Not ready? Not bloody ready? They sodding well should be! Pictures may still be worth a thousand words, but those words don't speak the truth anymore. They've had long enough to appreciate the work of cheap hacks like Picasso. Now they're must experience the full throttle excellence of Rollie Erlichman!" he said, waving his brush frantically.

"Yes I suppose so. I like it," I said, as I watched him put the brush down next to the colour palette.

"So. You and Trish seemed rather cosy this morning," he said.

"It wasn't what it looked like. I mean there was nothing..."

"Relax Maxwell, I was just pulling your leg. Trish told me about your little episode last night."

I felt a little embarrassed. I wasn't sure why.

"You really should see someone about those night-terrors."

"Yeah. Trish said the same thing. It wasn't too bad last night. There have been worse. Like the time I sleepwalked into the middle of a road," I said.

"Holy Moses!" replied Rollie. "You've never told me about that."

"There doesn't seem much point in drudging up bad stuff, you know?"

"Yeah. I know what you mean. I've never spoken to anyone about Korea. Not the ex-wife, not even Gina. Some things are best left undisturbed."

"You served in Korea?"

"No. Vacation. It was terrible," he said.

I almost choked on my tea. Rollie had the gift of great timing with his jokes.

"Seriously though, yeah, I was a medic. Some of what I saw, I don't think even hell itself could compare to it."

I didn't tell him about Bosnia.

"Yeah. Well like you said, best left undisturbed," I said.

"You know, you and Trish would fit well together I think."

"Come on, knock it off Rollie. Quit playin' matchmaker. Besides, she deserves better than someone like me."

"Well, I'm just saying."

"Yeah. Well, listen, thanks for your hospitality and everything dude. I really should get going though."

"Not a problem young man. I have to get over to the allotment myself later. Those tomatoes should be ripe enough to be plucked from the vines."

"Nothing better than a home grown red tomatoes," I added.

"Well they're not red. They're green. You know if you leave them in front of the window after picking them, they'll naturally turn red. Makes them juicier too."

"That I did not know," I replied

"Are you good for bus fare?"

"Yeah," I said. "I've got plenty of change."

I delved into my trouser pocket to make sure. I'd been caught short a few times and found myself without the necessary money. Twice the driver had taken pity on me and let me on free of charge, once he'd grabbed me by my collar to throw me off. It took me three hours to walk home that day and by the end of it, my legs were like jelly. I didn't want to take that risk again.

Gina and Rollie saw me to the door, bid me goodbye and thanked me again for loaning them the computer. I hopped down the stairs, re-energised with a new-found sense of optimism and sprung into street like a Canadian jack-rabbit. The bus was twenty minutes late. It wasn't like I had anywhere to be or any kind of important deadline, but I was buzzing with impatient energy and just wanted to get back to familiar territory.

I grabbed a newspaper from the bundle next to the drivers

cabin. The troubles in London were still making front page news, with grainy images of offenders splashed across almost every page. The story on page two read 'Olympic Ambassador Accused of Riot Attack'.

'A Teenage girl who is an Olympics ambassador hurled bricks at police during rioting in London this week. The teenager, described as a 'talented sportswoman' was caught on camera allegedly throwing bricks at a police car in Enfield, north London. The girl is one of the Olympic volunteers who put themselves forward to help out at the games next summer. She has met the London Mayor Boris Johnson, Olympics chief Sebastian Coe and visited the House of Commons. Her mother spotted her on a television broadcast and immediately called the police. She said the decision to report her daughter was 'gut-wrenching', adding 'I had to do what was right'. The teenager was refused bail and will appear in magistrates' court in five days time.'

23. The Lion, The Witch & The Warthog...

I got off at the stop near the Cessnock tube station. The wind was beginning to pick up. Heavy clouds blocked out the sun and I couldn't warm myself in its heat. I wasn't sure if it was going to rain or not. It wasn't unusual to see all four seasons in the space of a day.

The newspaper was wedged under my arm. I hadn't gotten around to the funny pages. The cartoon strips were always a treat. An antithesis to the sad caricatures in daily life. From the postman to the lollipop lady, all desperately trying to recapture the faded glory of their prime. For a brief moment, you saw a spark - a funny joke, words of wisdom - then lost again; back to the grindstone. Such willing servants of the state. Muddling through, getting by, eating more, drinking less; good sheepdogs obeying the whistle of the punch-clock.

Yesterday's news quickly became today's chip paper, smeared on garbage cans; the sickly smell of ketchup and rotting fish. I could see the dried stains from puke-ridden take-out trays, propped up against a lamp post on the blood-spattered pavement. The inevitable result of drunken arguments, multiple stab wounds and belligerent grown-ups defeated in the challenge of making it from dusk 'til dawn; unable to live, unwilling to die. Along came the street sweeper, wiping away the muck and sucking up the guts of local hard men who thought they'd have a go at spinning the wheel of fortune; try their luck. Their number was up. Old lottery tickets littered shop doorways.

I turned a corner and plodded along until I came upon Brand Street. There was a small delicatessen a few blocks to the left that served excellent coffee and terrific sandwiches, not that I was hungry, but I thought it only sensible to buy a few eats and treats for later. The man behind the counter was dressed in a white smock, gloves and a pork pie hat. I wasn't sure why, but I assumed it had something to do with hygiene rules. The health and safety fad, imported from America's compensation culture. People sued for anything they could; from hair in their hamburgers to catching syphilis from an airplane toilet seat.

In started in the eighties, during the Regan/Thatcher era, it'd been drilled into us, 'Greed Is Good'. There was no mention of the price of it all. No talk of the pitfalls. The human cost had been completely ignored. The yuppies had been bred for financial warfare and were armed with trouser braces and a Filofaxes. But here we were, in 21st Century Britain, where privatised utility companies could legally charge record prices for our energy needs. There was no competition, no upside for the ordinary working man, though we'd been told it would be 'good for Britain'. Whoever controlled wholesale prices controlled the world. The old and infirm were hit hard each winter, unable to afford to pay their bills. It was extortion plain and simple. Many tried to avoid the costs by going without heating in the extreme cold. The ever increasing number of fatalities should have concerned us as a country. But then, we were too busy trying to keep the wolf from the chancellors door. Straw houses for straw men, easily blown down by the huffing, puffing big suits in sheep's clothing. In the past, we got through the tough times by tightening our belts. But the children of the modern age had been weaned on the tit of avarice. They were used a life of excess. Can't eat what's on your plate? Throw it away. Your shirt's out of style? Buy another one.

And why not? Seriously wealthy executives flew around in private jets and sailed in luxury yachts with their wives and mistresses. Was it such a sin that the less well off wanted a taste of the same? For the better part of twenty years, it had become customary for the fat cats to offer drippings to the poor. And we put them to good use. Nike and Lacoste were our answer to their Versace and D&G. They drank the finest sixty year old single malts, we enjoyed supermarket brand poly blends. They hired expensive hookers with supermodel looks, we were happy with streetwalkers who gave every customer a dose of the clap free of charge. Yes, my friends, we got the better end of that deal. We didn't have to worry about the market value of our stock portfolios; or think about being caught with our pants down in the middle of a secretarial fuck session. We were already being raped by the rich and powerful. Our pants were firmly lodged around our ankles and we knew damned well we had no hope of ever pulling them back up.

"Do you want mayonnaise on this chicken sandwich?" asked the guy behind the counter.

"Huh? Oh yeah. Can you add in some onions, tomatoes and lettuce?" I replied.

"Sure. Anything else?"

"Oh yeah, a cup of coffee to go too please."

"What kind?"

"Just a regular coffee. Lots of cream, lots of sugar."

"No problem. That'll be three fifty."

I took out a new five pound note from my wallet, feeling the porous paper between my fingertips. It seemed a shame to have to spend it. Crisp notes were a rarity, especially ones issues from the Bank of England. The queen's face stared up at me disapprovingly as I handed him the money. He counted out the change into my palm and gave me the sandwich, wrapped in several sheets of greaseproof paper. The coffee machine spluttered before letting out a stream of hot coffee. I watched him pour in the cream and seal the polystyrene cup. He threw me some sachets of sugar and I stuffed them into my back pocket.

I headed back to Cessnock. The underground was the

logical option. There was no sense in walking home. I went through the turnstiles and down the escalator. A few minutes later, a gust of air hit me and I saw two bright lights emerging from the dark tunnel. I stepped into the middle compartment and sat. The train jutted forward. Three stops later, I arrived at Govan.

There was a bus stop directly outside the station. Several people were already gathered there, also intent on catching the same bus. The driver got annoyed by my fumbling for change. I paid him and scrambled toward the middle of the bus, taking a seat next to the emergency exit.

A fat old Arab woman hobbled aboard and spoke curtly to the driver while a young fair-haired lass waited patiently behind. The girl struggled to find space for her guitar case. The older woman sat beside her. She seemed agitated. The prune faced hag snorted and spewed forth a slew of verbose utterances, which were I could tell were not polite because of her demeanour and tone. The girl appeared to be deeply offended, especially at the few sparse words of English that were mixed in. "British" and "prostitute" stood out and were enough to light the fuse on an already volatile situation. The girl exploded with an angry tirade of her own, laced with shocking profanity in true Glaswegian form. This dual between dialects continued for the better part of ten minutes. I could understand the girl's frustrations. She was dealing with a sort of reverse racism. The rest of us quietly watched the spectacle of a bloated warthog crushing a weaker piglet, who by then was on the verge of crying.

It was a most unfair situation, to be sure. But I'd witnessed similar scenes before. When I was about thirteen, an acquaintance of my father's visited our home and persuaded me to attend a presentation by a Muslim preacher at a local mosque. He felt it would 'cleanse my soul of its impurity'. I'd always been prone to the delights of wine, women and song and these were all strictly forbidden by Islamic law. I went along to the supposed seminar to learn a little about my father's belief system. Instead what I got was a treatise on the evils of Jews. I promptly left; disgusted by the debased teachings of what should have been a great pathway to enlightenment. It was, after all, a faith that counted great men like Bulleh Shah and Nusrat Fateh Ali Khan among its numbers. Yet according to the Imam, I, by default, had to hate my own mother because she was Jewish, and this contradicted one of the fundamental tenants of both religions; honour thy father and thy mother. I was more than aware that I was not personally living up to that with my wayward behaviour, but to be told by power mad preachers that you should pray for the destruction of all Jews because 'God willed it' seemed stupid; even to my young and impressionable mind. But this sort of poison was being injected into the brains of countless kids in many places. In Israel, Jewish children were being taught to hate Palestinians; In America, extremist Christians were teaching their progeny to hate Muslims; and in Britain, all of them were teaching hatred towards atheists.

The two women were still bickering on the bus and in all the excitement, I missed my stop. I thought about getting off at the next one, but I remembered that we would be passing by Braehead shopping centre. I needed a new pair of shoes, so I stayed on. My red converse sneakers were worn out and liable to come apart at an inopportune moment. This would not have been good. Running around the city barefoot was not a smart thing to do. Broken beer bottles were laying in wait at every corner and outside every pub. Once, I'd stepped on a shard by accident when, in a drunken frenzy, I ran across a road without any footwear; all for the sake of a dare. The twenty pounds I won was no recompense for the three weeks I spent limping, shot up with every drug known to man. Then there was the battery of tests, tetanus shots and indestructible titanium crutches. I felt like Lee

Majors; the Six Million Dollar Man.

By the time we reached the mall, the girl had was ready to flee. She'd turned bright pink and I could almost see the steam coming out of her ears. I was worried that her head might pop off her shoulders in a David Cronenberg styled display of animated intensity. I hung back until she was long gone before I too left the toxic atmosphere aboard the bus.

I could see the car park, full of large automobiles. People were rushing from all directions, going... somewhere. I bopped up to the big glass revolving door and breezed through to the air-conditioned sanctum of consumerism. 'Sale' signs were plastered across windows and even inside the stores. At the end of the walk of death, stood the mega chain that produced cheaply priced clothing and footwear. Sweatshop child labour was giving us bargain basement prices on quality goods. I wasn't going to complain about it; necessity took precedence over moral outrage. Hanging up, next to a pair of Batman pyjamas, were a pair of black converse trainers, at the reasonable discounted price of five pounds. My five pounds would go toward the £500 trillion debt we'd racked up on the national credit card. I was single-handedly saving the economy and it felt great.

The cashier rung it up and put the shoes into a large brown paper bag. The workers here didn't appear to be any more content with their day jobs than their counterparts in central Asia. Living corpses with robotic responses. Most were students, stuck in dead-end no-brain positions to afford that prized education. That was the toll they had to pay to get into the fast lane, next to Easy Street, where greased up geese laid five figure golden eggs. But these were pie-in-the-sky notions that would see them churning out till receipts for eternity. Like Burmese whores past retirement age, they'd be turning tricks for six quid an hour until they got too old. Then someone else would take over. Move over Jack, there's new kids on the block; come on old timer, make room for the next batch of snot-nosed gremlins. I looked up at the pimple faced kid and he stared back at me with empty eyes.

"Your change, sir. Next!" he shouted.

I walked away, not completely satisfied, but I'd gotten what I wanted. Wham. Bam. Thank you sir. A security guard was hovering over the men's clothing section like a squirrel clutching its nuts. I adjusted my belt buckle and passed through the detectors. I had nothing to fear. I was, after all, a paying customer. But sometimes the alarm went off for no good reason and it was all too easy for an innocent bystander to end up in a holding cell for shoplifters. This didn't happen and I was glad to be spared the ordeal of going to jail without passing go.

It was strange. Courts across the country were releasing the guilty with little more than a slap on the wrist and maybe, at worst, a little prison time. Behind bars you had access to a colour television, three square meals and a warm dry cell with an en-suite bathroom. Corporations were not so humane. In the eyes of their fine-lens cameras, you were guilty until you proved your innocence. Their vision was focused on the bottom line. All that beautiful money in off shore bank accounts.

And the banks? Ah, the banks. Ethereal entities that could deny you the right to your life-savings at the stroke of a pen. By their will, you were penalised for small transgressions. If you had a mortgage, they could take away your house and banish you to the lower rungs of the economic ladder. They had proclaimed themselves as gods in the place of Nietzsche's 'superman'. The laws of man couldn't change the commandments that came from up on high. It didn't matter that they held shares in the morally ambiguous territory of the arms trade, or that they laundered money for foreign governments intent on killing their own people. If Christ were alive today, he'd have struggled to toss the money changing temple tables. Maybe he'd be a computer hacker, crashing their systems anonymously. The banks were the face of El Diablo, on billboards and commercials everywhere; no longer hidden or possible to exorcise. These god-heads demanded our worship and our money. They made Dick Turpin look like an amateur.

On leaving the store, I was greeted by a man holding a bucket and a badge. A friendly enough soul, but he was intent on getting a small donation from my cash-strapped self. I explained to him that I was one step away from chronic alcoholism and had no money to waste on charitable acts. I was tempted to quote a line from Dickens on work houses and orphanages, but instead I said, "Look man, stop pestering decent people. Rob the rich if you must, but don't feed on the poor."

This startled him as he was not used to this manner of direct speech. These kinds of fuckers were used to guilt-tripping ordinary working people with pictures of poverty stricken children suffering from malnutrition in the third world. But I'd *lived* it. It wasn't anyone's fault except for the economic powers and despotic dictators, who had created the vile problem in the first place. In theory, they should have been the ones to put it right. Of course, since they had no intentions of doing so, it fell to us, the regular citizens to do something about it. Yet harassing the regular rag-tag team of shopping addicts wasn't really the answer. Folk like this bearded do-gooder meant well, but I couldn't help feeling that their attention was misdirected.

In his mind, I was Satan incarnate for fobbing him off. He probably even wished that I'd be struck down by some preternatural karmic force. It took a lot of guts to do something about the horrors of this world and I admired him for that. I personally had never felt the obligation to do so. What I'd seen of human beings was nothing short of stomach churning. Vice and wretchedness everywhere, in everyone. I'd often wished that we as a species would be obliterated by some passing comet or other. The only other thing in nature that took delight in the destruction and pain of others for the sake of its own survival was the single-celled microbial virus.

I left him to ponder these matters and continued on my way. The jewellery shops in the middle of the shopping centre had obscenely priced trinkets on display. Wedding rings, pendants and earrings, all waiting for the rapacious masses to scoop them up for the sole purpose of plundering their dearly beloveds most private recesses. This was how love was bought and sold in the world of the modern age. But had it always been that way? Lust and gluttony disguised in the purity of romance? 'Unconditional' love with terms and conditions in the small print of the sales brochure; the marriage certificate. Couplings made and broken in an instant for pastures new, where the grass was greener, the field fuller. All for the magpie love of shiny slivers of gold and silver.

"Would you like some help sir?" asked the woman behind me. Her svelte figure and bunched brunette hair made her a desirable choice of saleswoman. I was tempted to ask her to show me her wares, but I couldn't have afforded her expensive services. Although a quick glimpse wouldn't have been out of the question. The richer the woman, the more exotic her tastes.

"I was just looking," I replied. "Actually, perhaps you *can* help me... When do you knock off for lunch? "

"Well I was normally take my break around now. Why?"

"I was hoping you might want to grab something to eat."

"I have a boyfriend."

"So? It's just lunch"

"I really shouldn't..." she said. "Okay. You're buying?"

"Always." I replied.

24. Melt Through My Fingers...
Burn Baby, Burn...

The food court was packed. The strong smell of greasy meat wafted through the air and the sound of sizzling deep fat fryers bounced off the hollow walls. Toddlers and their siblings were squealing in high pitched whale songs. Sweat poured from the brows of the hard working staff. The queue was growing ever longer. All these useless eaters, expecting them to put the 'fast' into fast-food. My lady friend and I got to the front. The girl taking orders looked as though she'd been savaged in a house of ill-repute. The manager in the white shirt busied himself watching the fries crackle in the hot oil, twitching nervously like a man close to embarking on a shooting spree because his chips were undercooked.

My companion couldn't make up her mind, so I ordered a quarter-pounder with cheese for her, along with a tasty beverage and fries. We sat down and I watched her scoff the lot down in a matter of minutes. I'd barely unwrapped my sandwich by the time she'd finished. My coffee was stone cold, but I drank it anyway. This was not the most romantic of settings, but we weren't there to embark on the affair of the century. Our plans revolved around some fast love to go with the fast-food. She was quiet. Was it was possible that she wasn't aware of my ulterior motives? Did she really just think this was an innocent lunch?

"So, what got you into the jewellery trade?" I asked.

"I saw an ad for a sales-assistant and I applied. I love being around pretty sparkly things."

She didn't seem like a stuck up rich bitch. In fact, she came across as a decent, down to earth sort of woman, the kind you could pick out curtains with on a Saturday afternoon. She'd learned to mimic the traits of a high society girl, prim and proper;

probably to attract a mate above her station. The female of the species is more deadly than the male.

Posh chicks turned me on. I found them to be the most debauched due to their sexually repressed upbringing. But this one was a mystery. She could go either way; an easily excitable damsel of devilish delight, or a mouthy maiden who might swear like a sailor in heat.

"You know, you have the most delectable lips. I'll bet they taste like peach ice-cream. Would you let me have a little lick?"

"You shouldn't say things like that. I've told you already, I'm with someone,"

She didn't seem cross, nor did she leave in disgust. My instincts were proving to be correct.

"Of course you are dear-heart. But is it so terrible to explore the realms of possibility?"

"I can't believe I'm even doing this!"

"Doing what? Having lunch?"

"You know fine well! I don't even know your name. Mine is..."

"No. No names. Why spoil something special?"

By this point we were both feeling the electric lightening between our thighs. She squeezed my shoulder, stood up and took a step toward me. I circled around her and kissed the nape of her neck before whispering sweet nothings into her ear.

We were all too aware that a public display of our wicked perversions would have been extremely indiscreet. She took me by the arm and pushed me into a service elevator. They used it to transport stock between floors. The doors closed. There was no escape. Without warning, she pulled the emergency stop and latched onto my waist, peppering my chest with kisses. I responded in kind, almost ripping the clothes from her slim body. In a matter of moments I was penetrating her. She panted heavily in-between screaming obscenities that would have made Hugh Hefner blush. Soon the two of us were engulfed in orgasmic pleasure and become lost in the rush of heart-pounding delectation. I came, she arrived then she sank into the corner. A few minutes later, she composed herself, got dressed and stood there sulking. She dared not look at me for fear of recognising her morally reprehensible actions.

When the doors re-opened, we found ourselves facing three store clerks standing next to a pallet truck. Had we been caught 'In flagrante delecto'? It was difficult to say. She got out and ran back to work.

Power was indeed an aphrodisiac. The whole time that she thought we were strangers, I'd read her name tag and knew more about her than she did of me. Knowledge was power and power corrupted. The supposed commitment to her relationship, her protestations of having a boyfriend, all came to nothing. Her desires melted through my fingers. I'd allayed her fears, telling her that I was just a guy; a ship passing through the night; but not her man. He needn't know a thing about it.

Sated and calmed, I leaned against the window of the hand-made soap store and changed into the black converse sneakers I'd bought earlier. They still had that pleasant new shoe smell. I threw the old ones in a nearby trash can and walked out of the shopping mall. It occurred to me that there might have been a camera in the lift. Had we provided some overweight doughnut munching security guard with jerk-off material, destined for his bulging private collection?

Across from the main complex was the largest computer store in the city. They sold everything from hard drives and miscellaneous components to whole built machines. I thought it a good idea to take a look and report any bargains to Rollie. The laptop I'd lent him was old and decrepit, a relic of twentieth century engineering. He needed a proper replacement, something contemporary, with a processor speed made Einstein look like a high school physics student.

The shop was nothing more than a glamorised warehouse, but it made you feel like you'd walked through a portal into the future. Giant wall mounted LCD television screens with non-stop ads in a never ending loop. Time stood still here. Fancy glass cabinets showcased the newest high-tech fads, stretching out as far as the eye could see, each aisle dedicated to a specific product line. The speed at which superfluous items were being brought to market was shocking. Most were absolutely unnecessary but came with a steep price tag. All that cash going toward worthless shit instead of going towards helping our brother man.

They were the ultimate in spinal crackers; fashionable must haves for the ordinary worker, who bent over backwards to purchase them. The perfect customer, with his head so far up his own ass that proctologist would recommend immediate surgery. Cut out the cancer. But how? There was no escape. The exits weren't marked and even the check-out desks were blocked with automated bars. You *had* to buy something. You didn't *need* any of it. But that was okay. Advertising created the artificial demand necessary. Was this what freedom had come to mean?

I spent the remainder of my incarceration desperately searching for a way out, seeing rows of sameness over and over and over again. What would Rollie make if it all? How would he choose? Why was I even attempting to gather information on these hideously complicated things? It was entirely possible that at his age, he would have a seizure from this kind of sensory overload.

One fellow, kitted out in company uniform, came over and offered to help. An old guy with nicotine stained fingers and bad breath. I asked him to tell me which of these machines was the undisputed king of the technological jungle.

"Well sir," he said. "I don't think there is any computer in here that's necessarily *better* than the others. I could show you the latest one that just came in today. It's at the high end of the spectrum in terms of speed, power and reliability. It's a newer model from the one you were just looking at. Would you like to see it?"

"Sure," I said. "But do you have one that would do everything it does for less?"

"Ah, you're a shrewd man aren't you!" he said. "But before I answer your question, can I ask, what sort of budget are we working with?"

We? *We* weren't working with any budget. What was he going to do? Offer his pay-check toward the cost?

"Well, I'm not actually looking to buy today. I was in the mall and thought I'd pop in and take a gander for a friend."

"Oh," he said, disheartened by my response. "If you just wait here one moment, I'll get someone who'll be able to help you with that."

'Rude bastard,' I thought. It was obvious what had happened. He realised he wasn't going to get his bonus today and decided to pawn me off to one of his colleagues. It all came down to pounds and pennies. First, they persuaded you to buy the most expensive item they could sell you and then they'd try to slide in the 'optional' insurance policy that had more holes in it than a tree infested with woodworm.

I waited another fifteen minutes, but no-one else came to my aid. Sure that no-one was looking; I made my dash into the open air. Free at last. There was a travel information booth not too far away with a dedicated phone for local taxis. I watched a cavalcade of cars circling the car park, the drivers all praying to the parking-space angel in humbled mantras for an empty slot for their immaculately washed automobiles. The rising cost petrol and insurance made it impractical to have one. And there never any guarantee that you wouldn't be towed away by some bitter old spinster of a traffic warden, who'd chosen your car after sensing its sexually magnetic properties.

The lady in the information booth twiddled her hoop earrings while she jabbered away to her boss He was a portly fellow with a white moustache and some strange stains on his trousers. I quizzed the woman in the booth on bus routes and timetables. She chewed on her gum while her eyes scrolled down the screen in front of her. The overhead halogen lamps shone off her skin. She'd applied too much make up that morning and her face looked like a prosthetic mask.

"There's two buses that would take you where you want to go. There's the twenty-three and a wee local twenty one, but that terminates at Govan"

"Thanks," I said.

I waited at the bus shelter. Voracious shoppers came and went and a few sat down next to me with bags full of goodies. I could see the clouds gathering in the horizon and the sky was getting darker. It was set to rain again. A young man next to me asked me for the time.

At 4.15pm the local bus showed up. Five other bling sporting teenagers got on, burdened with their newly bought belongings which would now help them feel that they did indeed belong. They were part of the greater galaxy, the in-crowd. Generation Y was conforming to the preconceived edicts of old. Eat, drink and be merry. Fuck everyone else, shag them silly, dance the merry jig round the mulberry bush. Why fight the future? Flow with it, go with it, get loose, live big, die hard.

The rain splattered in thick specks against the Perspex window. I tried to blank out the conversations. In the space of seven minutes, I'd learned all about some girl called Janice, her troubles with her step-father and something about her grandmother's false teeth. Thankfully, I arrived at my stop. I lit up a cigarette and smoked it under the cover of a tree. An old man and his dog strode past. While the owner was busy talking on his phone, his pet poodle grabbed a few stolen moments of whorish leg-humping with my left shin. I looked up at him, but he seemed unconcerned. I was sure he knew exactly what his four legged friend was doing. He just didn't want to accept the ugly truth of it. Or maybe he did. Maybe he even encouraged it. But why was the dog fucking my leg? Did it on some level sense the mongrel mutt in me? Did it know that I was a kindred spirit, an entity of so many parts that no singular segment defined the whole; half animal, half man?

The man and his scrotal licking friend left quickly. I stubbed out my cigarette butt and strolled toward my flat. I noticed a post-marked envelope wedged in my letterbox. The postman must have been. With the lack of mail in recent days, I wondered if he'd taken a sabbatical from his steadfast duties.

There was no return address on the back. I felt a strange sensation in the pit of my stomach and knew that its contents weren't likely to be good. I didn't typically receive letters like this. Most were official, bills or pay-cheques. I tore it open slowly, preparing myself for bad news.

"Dear Max,

Writing this letter has been the hardest thing I've had to do for a long time. I don't quite know how to tell you this, so I'll just come out and say it. I've met someone. Someone wonderful who makes me laugh and sing with joy. You were special. I mean that. Please don't call or write. I'm happy now.

Luv Kandy."

I felt a blow to my chest. It hit hard. I couldn't breathe. I was dizzy, light-headed. It took me a few moments to regain my strength. The incredible pain was still there. Little did I know it would remain there. My throat was suddenly dry and I was struggling to think straight, to unscramble my thoughts. I moved into the living room and slumped down on the couch. I reached for the bottle of Southern Comfort on the table. It consoled my troubled mind.

Some say it's better to have loved and lost. They've have never really loved at all. Not with their whole heart and soul. The loss of love was no less bitter a pill than the loss of a loved one to the open arms of death. The same people say time heals all wounds. They never mention how slowly the second hand ticks for self-inflicted wounds of passion.

26. Golden Balls, Crazy Cats & a Handful of Hope...

A bottle of beer in one hand and a copy of Sports Illustrated Swimsuit magazine in the other. My eyes had dried over with a greenish yellow crust; the kind that only develops after twelve consecutive hours of hard drinking. I'd lost my wallet during the course of the previous evening. Some poor degenerate scum had likely stolen both of these to feed his heroin habit.

The mirror in the hallway scared me half to death. *Who* was that staring back at me? My facial hair had turned into a self sustaining forest, and my clothes reeked of weeks' worth of body odour. Had it really come to this? Had I actually debased myself beyond all imaginable levels?

My stomach was yo-yoing around my ankles. I tried to find my nail clippers, but they were nowhere to be found. They wouldn't have been up to the challenge anyway. I grabbed a pair of kitchen scissors, lying amidst the empty pizza boxes and stale leftover crusts.

My hygiene standards had suffered dramatically as a result of the depression, and my flat looked like it had been invaded by storm troopers who'd used it as an unceremonious dumping ground. After doing some modest cleaning, I took a warm bath then checked the messages on my answering machine. I skipped through the cold calling sales patter from double glazing companies and personal injury experts. Finally I came to a voice I recognised.

"Hey buddy. Hope you're okay. I haven't heard from you in ages. Give me a buzz when you can."

I dialled the Rabbi's number: 001-555-818-6620. It would be about morning there. If I was lucky, I'd catch him before he left for the gym. The phone kept ringing out. I thought of leaving a fiercely indecent voicemail. But I reneged when I heard the click on the other end.

"Glassman residence."

"Avi?"

"Max! Where've you been dude? I was shitting bricks thinking something terrible had happened to you."

"It did. I was kidnapped by a group of mountain dwellers who tortured me until I revealed the location of that secret stash of yak's milk."

"You didn't tell them, did you?"

"No. But they may come looking for you. They *knew* I was going to send it to you!"

"Oh God! Why Lord, why?"

"I guess they had intelligence. The CIA must have been in on it! Why, they're probably listening to us right now."

"Don't say things like that man."

"Sorry. I would've called sooner, but I was on a despicable downer."

"The girl?"

"Yeah."

"Damn. I'm sorry man. If it makes you feel any better, things are rough here too."

"How so?"

"Well my accountant finally decided to file a Chapter 11."

"A Chapter 11?"

"Yeah. Bankruptcy. It was the only option. Not sure what's going to happen with the house yet."

"Damn. I'm sorry to hear that."

"Don't be. It's for the best I think. The Lord's way of telling me to be one of my flock and focus on my destiny."

"Well, I'm a great believer in looking at the bright side."

"Listen, I don't want to cut this short, but I have to pack the little man's lunch and do the school run."

"No problemo. I'll catch you when I catch you. Take it easy Avi."

I felt bad for the Rabbi. There he was, in the middle of losing everything, and I'd been moaning about some slut. All things considered, I wasn't doing too badly. But I still needed some fresh air and the company of those afflicted with a similar melancholy.

By mid afternoon I was safely ensconced in the Scotia Bar on Stockwell Street. It was like a second home. It made me feel like I was back in the womb, within the familiar folds of a dysfunctional family. Maybe it was the rustic charm of the panelled woodwork; maybe it was the large selection of in-house ales. Colin greeted me in his typical warm manner.

Colin was one of the bar-staff, a real stand up individual who'd perhaps spent too much of his time listening to me whine on certain Saturday nights before inevitably hideous Sunday mornings.

"You're usual?"

"No. Guinness."

"Coming right up."

He pulled a pint and left it to settle on the drainer. There was nothing worse than taking a gulp from an unsettled pint of Guinness. I glanced over at the suit next to me who had his eyes glued to his latest gadget. He was toying that iPad like it was his girlfriend's cunt, moving his fingers up, down, side to side and then stopping because his hand got tired. He was wearing a tag identifying him as a clerk from the Sheriff Court. He had that look about him; of a jaded man who'd wasted his precious hours in the company of too many contemptible villains.

I glanced over his shoulder as he trawled the Google news links on the touchscreen in his hand. The Bank of England was revising its forecasts, the dollar had been downgraded, losing its triple A rating, and the Euro was hurtling towards an imminent collapse.

Doughnuts cooked in black oil in American bakeries, ready for export to nations far and wide, were going to cost that little bit more. But I couldn't bring myself to truly give a fuck about it. Not one single, solitary raccoon's ass of a fuck. We'd all rolled the dice once too often. Snake eyes had to come up sometime. Every sensible gambler knows that you have to learn to lose when you play to win. It was time to let it go. We weren't the first to spring up on this godforsaken rock, but we appeared to be doing everything possible to make sure we'd be the last.

The barfly at the other end of the bar slammed down his pint.

"This's been such a fucked up year hasn't it?" he shouted.

"Yeah," I said.

"You couldn't make any of this bollocks up! It's just a complete shit storm."

The suit moved away, unwilling to engage in any kind of discourse with the likes of us. We probably offended him with our presence.

"Posh git," muttered the barfly.

Colin brought over my Guinness and I sipped on it, nursing it for as long as I could. He added the cost to my running tab. We'd gotten into the habit of me racking it up as high as it would go and then paying it off at the end of the year. It had become a sort of ritual.

Maggie, the landlady who ran the joint, brought over a plate of food and I ravenously devoured the steak and chips while she sat there staring at me. She put on her glasses and folded her arms.

"You look a little green around the gills. Is everything alright?"

"Yeah. Everything's fine," I said. "I've just been a little under the weather."

"I like the beard. It suits you."

She went back behind the bar and I looked through the leaflets sitting in bundles beside the wet coasters. There was one in particular that got my attention.

Sister Stevens
Psychic Reader & Gifted Healer
The Most Accurate Readings.
I have come here to help the suffering.
½ Price 30 Minute Sessions Limited Time Offer.
Call To Arrange An Appointment:
0141 110 1010

I stuffed it into my pocket and ordered a tall glass of Coca-Cola. I watched the game that was on the flat-screen television.

This was one of the Old Firm matches that the commentators often referred to as the Glasgow Derby. It was a clash between titans. Rangers FC pitted against their greatest adversaries in the known galaxy; Celtic FC. Rangers had previously won three Scottish Premier League titles in succession, and they held a four point advantage over their arch rivals. But in the last season, Celtic had cleaned up pretty well, picking up the majority of points in the Old Firm league games; though they did not win the championship. Rangers FC also had the added woe of having serious financial troubles that threatened to take down the club. They needed another win to boost their moral.

No easy chances were taken or given by either side in the opening half. Three precision targeted attempts at securing victory yielded results. With each goal came the cacophony of celebratory screaming. It took Rangers midfielder and striker Steven Naismith to break the initial deadlock, and he delivered his first successful attack, after returning Kevin Wilson's clearance with terminal intensity. Striker Gary Hooper, an emboldened Englishman with an equally unstoppable hard-on for scoring on and off the pitch, restored parity for Celtic. But there was another harsh sting in the tail awaiting Rangers. Allan McGregor, goalkeeper and resident half-wit of the day, allowed the ball to slip right out from his hands, following a long shot Hail Mary volley from Moroccan born Left Back, Badr El Kaddouri. At half-time, Rangers' manager Ali McCoist made it a personal point to praise McGregor for his performance last season. But it had clearly escaped his attention that *this* was not last season.

The second half did not start well. Rangers Forward Kyle Lafferty 'equalised', only to have his efforts discounted because of the offside rule. He then threw away two opportunities to make up for his initial foul-up. This caused some panic in the trenches. Celtic Centre Back, Glenn Looves, kept his cool and went deep behind enemy lines with the intention of shooting his arsenal of explosive footwork into the back of the net. But his well played header met with an immovable goal post, thwarting him and sending him deep into despair. Lafferty still managed to prove his worth after firing the inflated missile of a football past the goalposts and secured the lead for Rangers in this testosterone fuelled frenzy.

The fans in both stands went wild, cheering, hissing, booing and baying for blood. This was all out war, two tribes slugging it out for the win. Celtic's aspirations were laid to rest after Brown's injury and a red card send off for Mulgrew put another nail in the coffin. The final seal on the death of the SPL dream came when Naismith swooped down with great vengeance and again delivered a fantastic end score for McCoists team. Rangers fans celebrated their 4-2 success, while their Celtic counterparts sat in pubs across Glasgow, intent on drowning in their sadness.

On game days, there was always trouble. I decided to wait until it died down. The Scotia had no ties to either team and was considered neutral ground; akin to holy ground in the film Highlander.

A stack of bundled newspapers lay on the table behind me. I thumbed through one. The small caption on page twelve caught my eye. There was a police crackdown on yet another peaceful demonstration, in another part of the world. The Occupy movement was not faring well. The barbarity of the beatings and tear gas attacks on people exorcising their constitutional rights was revolting. It left no difference between America, Syria, Libya, or Iran. It roused in me a deep fury that I was sure was going to boil over and make me into a font of misplaced rage. The photographs were abysmally heinous. Women and children were being mauled in ways that not even a Bengal tiger would dare. When several of the protesters walked into a branch of a local bank to demand their money, they were either ejected or locked in, and experienced the full wrath of hired goons and plain clothes detectives, conspiring to create mass mayhem, and hoping that their efforts would force the hippy bastards to evacuate the makeshift camps they'd set up.

This kind of crazed badness was too much for me. I entertained the idea of cryogenics; freezing myself and becoming an immortal human icicle - at least until we overcame these doom-struck days. However, there was a serious drawback to the plan. It would quite probably hamper my sex-life, and that did not make it an appealing prospect. I dismissed the notion as quickly as it had entered my mind, finished off my coke and grabbed my leather jacket. I remembered there was a gig due to start at 9pm at Pivo, a place that regularly featured live new bands. I had a little time to kill so I went outside, lit up a cigarette and took a walk around the block.

'Fuck it!' I thought. 'No sense in hanging around here.'

I walked up to Trongate then turned left onto Argyle Street, which was still mobbed with football freaks and uncouth sons of a thousand bitches, spitting and spewing over every one who crossed their path. There was no avoiding them. But my demeanour must have shown them that I wasn't prepared to put up with their level of infantile bullshit. They avoided me like the plague. These no good scum regularly terrorised the streets. They headed down into the guts of the Subway system, screeching like owls on a twilight hunt. I was rid of them. But what of the decent people who'd have to put up with them?

I took a left onto Waterloo street and right on the corner was Pivo. It was a sort of bar, restaurant and club, merged into one in a hideous underground bunker, serving imported beers with strange names. I suspected that it had originally been built as a fallout shelter. The bouncer nodded as I went in and I went downstairs where a large sandwich board announced 'Tina Taylor, for one night only: her music makes even manly men weep teers of joy.'

I ordered a bottle of Argentinian suds and sat down near the stage. A nasal speaking no-hoper at the next table leaned over and said something. I couldn't quite make it out at first.

"Awright pal. Yoo waint sum ae this?"

He flashed a baggie.

"Sure," I replied.

The freak of nature had just offered me smack. Heroin was not a recreational drug for addictive personalities. Its morphine like effects meant that it jacked itself into your system faster than spyware on a Russian horse porn website. The bouncer from outside walked toward me, and at first I was concerned that I was about to be thrown out. But instead, he grabbed the junkie dealer.

"I know you're dealing in here you little prick! Get the fuck out before I call the cops."

I watched the jaundiced druggie run like the wind. It was a shame he couldn't get clean. He may have done well in the upcoming London Olympics.

Tina Taylor appeared on stage. Her jet black hair flowed down past her shoulders. She had brown almond eyes that sparkled in the spotlight and made her irresistibly attractive. Her drummer laid down a 'phat' beat on the skins as she began strumming the guitar, serenading the microphone with the sweetness of her voice.

I spotted four female German students sipping Singapore Slings in the corner. There was enough alcohol in each glass to knock out a Bavarian Bull. They seemed like my sort of people so I went over and introduced myself. We bonded over our eclectic taste for the music of David Hasselhoff. They invited me back to their hotel room and I accepted. We rounded off the drinking session in their suite and as the night wore on, we become increasingly daring, participating in vile and sordid things that would have raised eyebrows in ancient Greece. But my destructive tendencies were also beginning to take hold. The mini-bar became a target for strange attacks with kitchen cutlery and the TV quickly met its end after committing suicide from the 14th floor. Before long, the girls were chasing me through the corridor, intent on stabbing me with a butter knife.

"We can't have guests trashing our premises in this manner!" screamed the concierge.

I bid my foreign friends farewell and roamed the streets for a while, thinking to pay the casino a visit. They had an all night liquor license. But instead I ran into a hobo near a convenience store and the two of us rocked out to Elvis Costello's greatest hits. I had to ditch him when he tried to lick my elbows.

At about 5am, I was overcome with the half-baked notion that I would try singing for loose change in a dimly lit alleyway. This proved successful and earned me six pounds in greasy coins, which was just enough for the cab ride home.

27. Super Psychic Shamanic Mysteries...

I fumbled in my pocket for the flyer I'd found at the bar. I called Sister Stevens in a drunken frenzy. I had a lot of tough questions that needed an answer.

'Why am I here? What the hell does it all mean? Is this the end of the road?

'I was just kidding Sister Stevens, just trying to test you out, see if you were the real deal. Why? Because I was leading up to this extremely important question. What? No, I'm not nervous. Where am I from? Way up north where people's testicles freeze seven months out of the year. Huh? Well, no, I've never had a psychic consultation before. What? Well, the awful truth of it is that I've been feeling extremely weary this past month. What? Now, wait a minute, I still haven't gotten to what I wanted to ask... Eh? No, I don't think I did... Yes, I am Scottish... No, let's not get into that. Just let me ask you this question – and I mean this very seriously - if I slash my wrists with this broken beer bottle, will I finally be rid of all the pain?'

But I didn't ask that. Instead a gentle voice answered on the other end.

"This is Sister Stevens. Can I have your name?"

"Max."

"And what can I do for you Max?"

"There are things I need to know. What can you tell me?"

"Spirit tells me that you're in great sorrow. There's a sadness in you isn't there?"

"There is," I replied.

"Yes, it runs deep."

I recognised immediately that this was a cold reading. Another cheap hack trying to make a quick buck off desperate souls in despair. But I carried on listening.

"This is because of a girl isn't it? I can see that she caused you a lot of anguish."

"Yes."

"Let me do a tarot spread here for you too."

"Okay. If you think that would help."

She shuffled around and I heard strange noises on the other end. Then, a scream.

"Sorry. The cards fell out of my hands. I want you to brace yourself. There's some bad news here."

"Fire away."

"This girl isn't coming back into your life. She's left for good. I know that's probably the last thing you want to hear. But I always tell people what I see."

"Yes. I know."

"There's also a card here I need to tell you about. But before I do, I must explain that you can't take the names of the cards literally."

"I understand."

"You have the Devil card as your signifier."

"What does that mean? That I'm Satan or something?"

"No. It means that you're under the influence of dangerous energies. You have to be careful not to indulge in vice."

"Right..."

"You also have to avoid negative thinking patterns. There's a real danger of falling into that."

"Ah."

"The death card is also present. Now, I must stress, that does not mean that you're going to die."

"So what does it mean?"

"That you're going to go through a process of rebirth. You're going to put the past behind you, bury it and move forward into a new phase of your life."

"Okay," I said, incredulously.

"Let me look into my crystal ball."

"You have a crystal ball?"

"Yes. I'm from a Romany gypsy family."

"I see."

"There's a great deal of change coming your way. A fresh start abroad, an opportunity you weren't expecting. Do you gamble?"

"Occassionally."

"You're going to win something. Hmm… This is interesting. Are you a creative individual Max?"

"Not really."

"I can see you writing something. Have you ever considered writing a book?"

"No. I don't think I could."

"Perhaps you should think about it. This is so strange. I keep getting Paraguay. Have you ever been there?"

"Afraid not. Nor do I have any plans to go there. I'm broke. I couldn't afford to even if I wanted to."

"That won't be the case for long."

"There's also going to be a new woman coming into your life."

"There have been many new women 'coming' into my life," I quipped.

"This is someone special."

"Well, I'm not holding out hope."

"What did I say about negative thinking?"

"Sorry. There is one thing I was wondering. With you being psychic and everything, you'll know"

"Ask away."

Well, I was wondering… where could I score some free acid?"

Dial tone.

Fucking Bitch! No help at all. I passed out next to the toilet clutching a bottle of household bleach. I woke around the time that the morning mail came. Among the usual bills there was a letter confirming an all expenses paid vacation. I'd entered a competition on the back of a box of cornflakes in April and had forgotten about it. The destination? Paraguay. I gave serious thought to writing a book.

END

Made in the USA
Charleston, SC
03 May 2012